SONNET 155

THE VELVET TONGUE

A Novel

by

Heather Hollis

SONNET 155: THE VELVET TONGUE

A Novel

ISBN *(Paperback)*: 978-X-XXXX-XXXX-X

Published by **Humbolton Press**
First Edition

Cover design: Heather Hollis
Interior design: Heather Hollis

Table of Contents

CHAPTER ONE: ***The Room That Didn't Fight Back*** 5

CHAPTER TWO: ***The Sound That Stayed*** 15

CHAPTER THREE: ***The Hand That Wrote Before*** 27

CHAPTER FOUR: ***The Invitation*** 37

CHAPTER FIVE: ***The Performance*** 49

CHAPTER SIX: ***The Ones It Cannot Reach*** 61

CHAPTER SEVEN: ***The One Who Broke*** 74

CHAPTER EIGHT: ***The Cost of Knowing*** 85

CHAPTER NINE: ***The Second Body*** 93

CHAPTER TEN: ***The Salon*** 100

CHAPTER ELEVEN: ***The Corrupted Version*** 108

CHAPTER TWELVE: ***The Conversation*** 114

CHAPTER THIRTEEN: ***The Fracture*** ..127

CHAPTER FOURTEEN: ***The Performer Breaks*** 133

CHAPTER FIFTEEN: ***Harris Unravels*** 140

CHAPTER SIXTEEN: ***The Night She Listened*** 148

CHAPTER SEVENTEEN: ***The Betrayal***
....157
CHAPTER EIGHTEEN: ***The Deal***..........164
CHAPTER NINETEEN: ***The Preparation***
....172
CHAPTER TWENTY: ***The Demonstration***..183
CHAPTER TWENTY-ONE: ***The Interruption***..190
CHAPTER TWENTY-TWO: ***The Fallout***
....196
CHAPTER TWENTY-THREE: ***The Choice***
....201
CHAPTER TWENTY-FOUR: ***The Altered Verse***...214
About the Author....................................224

CHAPTER ONE: *The Room That Didn't Fight Back*

The room showed no signs of struggle, and that was the first thing that bothered Lena Marchetti.

Detective Aaron Kline had said it like an apology when he stepped aside to let her through the doorway, "no signs of struggle", as if the absence itself were something she might trip over. She'd heard the phrase a thousand times in a dozen different precincts, from officers who thought it was a comfort. It never was. Rooms that didn't fight back were the ones that scared her.

She paused just inside the threshold, letting her eyes adjust not to the light but to the grammar of the space. That was how she'd described it once in a lecture at Columbia, back when she still did lectures, a room was a sentence written in objects, and her job was to find the broken syntax. Overturned furniture meant panic. Shattered glass meant explosive emotion. Bloodstains described trajectories and intentions in a language older than speech itself. Each element was a clause, and if you read them in the right order, the room would tell you what had happened.

This room told her nothing.

Books lined three walls from floor to crown molding in careful, obsessive symmetry. Not decorative. These were working shelves, margins bristling with colored tabs, spines cracked at habitual angles, annotations layered over annotations in a penmanship that grew tighter and more urgent as it moved deeper into the stacks. A scholar's den. The kind of room that smelled the way old libraries wished they did: paper and leather and the dry, mineral tang of ink that had been drying for decades.

A standing lamp in the corner cast warm light across a Persian rug that had seen better centuries. A window behind heavy curtains, closed. No draft. No disturbance. Even the dust motes hung motionless in the lamplight, as though the air itself had been told to hold still.

At the center of it all sat the body.

Professor Lionel Ashcroft remained upright in his leather desk chair, hands resting on the surface of the oak desk with a looseness that suggested someone had gently arranged them after sleep. His posture was almost elegant, spine aligned with the chair back, shoulders neither hunched nor rigid, chin slightly elevated as if he'd been considering something important and wanted a better angle on it. If not for the flat, unresponsive glaze of his eyes, he might have been mistaken for a man who had simply paused mid-thought and was waiting for it to find him again.

"Time of death?" Lena asked without turning around.

"Somewhere between nine and eleven last night," Kline said from the doorway. He was leaning against the frame with the practiced slouch of a man who'd learned that crime scenes went faster if he stayed out of the specialist's way. "Building security says his keycard was last used at six-fourteen p.m. No exit logged after that."

"Forced entry?"

"Negative. Door was unlocked when the graduate assistant found him this morning. Security system shows no breaches. Windows sealed." Kline paused, and she could hear him shift his weight. "No toxins found so far, but the deeper panels are still running."

Lena moved further into the room, her flats making no sound on the rug. She circled the desk slowly, maintaining the kind of focused distance an astronomer might give a star, close enough to study, far enough to see the whole shape. Her eyes moved over the body without lingering, cataloguing what was present, then, more importantly, what was missing.

No defensive wounds on the hands or forearms. No bruising around the throat or wrists. No petechial hemorrhaging in the sclera. No rictus of pain distorting the muscles of the face. No clenched jaw, no torn fingernails, no fabric twisted where hands had gripped or clawed.

Professor Ashcroft had not fought back either.

"Who found him?" she asked.

"Graduate assistant. Kid named Harris Cole. Came by around ten this morning to drop off revisions. Found the door unlocked, walked in, found him like this." Kline consulted his phone. "He's in a conference room downstairs. Shaken but cooperating."

Lena nodded absently, her attention drawn past the body to the desk itself. It was a heavy piece, solid oak, old enough that the surface had developed the kind of dark, glassy patina that only decades of use and polish could produce. Papers were stacked at the edges with a librarian's precision. A fountain pen rested in its stand, cap on, the nib dry. A half-finished cup of tea sat to the left, cold, a skin of tannin filming the surface.

And there, near the center of the desk, directly in front of Ashcroft's resting hands, was something else.

Lena leaned closer.

A line of text had been carved into the wood.

Not scratched. Not gouged. *Carved*, with the clean, deliberate precision of someone who had taken their time, who had known exactly what they wanted to say and had no intention of hesitating. The letters were even in depth and spacing, incised into the oak with a steadiness that suggested either great patience or absolute calm. There were no false starts, no corrected strokes, no signs that the hand holding the tool had trembled at any point during the process.

Lena read the words without touching them.

When breath becomes command, the body obeys.

The sentence sat in the polished wood as though it had always been there, as though the desk had been built around it. She read it again, silently, and something in her attention snagged. Not on the meaning, that was cryptic enough to file away for later. On the *shape* of the sentence. The way the syllables fell against each other. The way her internal voice, reading it for the second time, wanted to pause in specific places, wanted to breathe between *command* and *the*, wanted to land on *obeys* with a weight that the word alone didn't quite justify.

There was a rhythm to it.

Kline had moved into the room now, standing beside the bookshelves with his arms crossed, watching her the way he always watched her, with the cautious interest of a man who'd hired a translator and was trying to decide whether to trust the translation.

"We checked for tools," he said. "Nothing in the room that could have made a cut that clean. No blade, no chisel, no X-Acto knife. Whatever did that isn't here."

"Or was taken," Lena said.

"Or was taken," Kline agreed. "But here's the thing, no hesitation marks. Whoever carved that knew exactly what they were writing before they started. One pass. No corrections."

Lena glanced back at the line. "Or had time to think about it."

Kline let out a slow breath. "Yeah. That's the part I don't like."

She turned her attention back to the body. Death had a vocabulary of its own, and Lena had spent her career learning to read it, not through autopsy reports and toxicology screens, which told you what had happened to the machine, but through the subtler language of posture, expression, and the tiny muscular details that most investigators walked right past.

She stepped closer to Ashcroft and studied his face.

Up close, the illusion of peace fractured, not into violence or pain, but into something more unsettling. His features were relaxed in a way that didn't match any cause of death she'd encountered in twelve years of consulting. The small muscles around his eyes, the orbicularis oculi, which contracted involuntarily during distress and were nearly impossible to consciously control, showed no evidence of strain. The corrugator supercilii above his brows, which would have furrowed during pain or confusion, lay smooth and undisturbed.

His expression wasn't neutral. It was specific.

Relief.

Not joy. Not fear. Not the blankness of sudden cardiac failure or the frozen surprise of an embolism. Relief, the kind that softened the entire architecture of the face, as though a great weight had been lifted in the final moments and the body had recorded that lifting in the only language it had left.

"Cause of death?" she asked.

Kline shook his head. "That's the problem. Heart stopped, sure. But there's no trigger. No blockage, no arrhythmia, no valve failure that the preliminary exam could find. It just stopped."

"Toxicology?"

"Clean so far. Like I said, deeper panels are running. But the ME's preliminary read is that everything looks normal." He paused. "Except for the part where he's dead."

Lena allowed herself a small, private smile at that. Kline's gift was his refusal to dress reality in anything but its own clothes. It was why she preferred working with him over the parade of detectives who tried to pre-digest their cases before handing them to her, as though her expertise made her too fragile for raw data.

She leaned closer to the body, focusing now on the details that fell within her particular domain. The jaw. The position of the tongue behind the teeth. The slight parting of the lips. The way the musculature of the throat had settled, not clenched, not strained, but aligned in a configuration she recognized from her research on vocalization patterns.

It was the posture of a mouth that had recently been open.

Not speaking. Not gasping. Not screaming.

Listening.

Ashcroft's entire body, from the relaxed hands to the slightly elevated chin to the open architecture of his throat, displayed the physical signature of receptive auditory focus. He had been listening to something in the moments before his death. Listening closely. Listening with his whole body, the way trained musicians and linguists did, not just with the ears but with the diaphragm, the jaw, the careful calibration of breath that allowed the body to become a more efficient receiver of sound.

"He was listening," she said.

Kline frowned. "Listening to what?"

"That's what we're here to find out."

She circled the desk one more time, slowly, letting her gaze move across the surface in a methodical grid.

The carved line pulled at her attention again, not because of what it said but because of what it *did*, the way it insisted on being read in a particular cadence, the way the internal stresses of the syllables created a pattern that felt less like prose and more like something designed. Engineered. Built to specifications she couldn't quite identify but could feel operating at the edges of her awareness, the way you could feel the bass line of a song through a wall without hearing the melody.

When breath becomes command, the body obeys.

She inhaled, not intentionally, not as a conscious act, but as a reflex triggered by the word *breath* meeting her eye at the same moment her lungs happened to be empty. A coincidence. Obviously a coincidence. But she noticed it, the way she noticed everything, and the noticing itself felt like a small, cold key turning in a lock she hadn't known was there.

"Lena?"

Kline's voice cut across her focus with the easy precision of a man who'd learned exactly how much volume it took to reach her when she was working.

She stepped back from the desk.

"His recent projects," she said, her tone returning to its clinical baseline. "What was he working on?"

Kline checked his notes. "Shakespeare, mostly. Historical phonetics. Something about the physical effects of Elizabethan verse structures, how specific rhythmic patterns in the original pronunciation might have had measurable physiological impacts on audiences."

Lena glanced at the bookshelves. Shakespeare folios. Prosody studies. Phonetic drift analyses. An entire wall dedicated to the architecture of sound.

"That's a fairly niche specialty," she said.

"Gets worse," Kline said. "Or better, depending on your definition. The graduate assistant mentioned that Ashcroft had gotten obsessive lately. Cancelled classes. Missed faculty meetings. Spent most of his time in here with the door locked." He gestured around the room. "Privacy request on file for the last three years, no security cameras, no audio monitoring inside the office."

"A man who studied language," Lena said, "and chose silence as his perimeter."

"I was going to say 'paranoid,' but sure, yours sounds better."

Lena turned back to the body one last time. Ashcroft sat in his chair as though he'd simply decided to stop, not in the violent, collapsed way of a heart attack, not in the confused, grasping way of a stroke, but with the deliberate, grateful stillness of someone who had reached the end of something and found that the ending was not what he'd feared.

Whatever had happened in this room had not left a mark on the body, the furniture, the walls, or the air. There was no evidence of intrusion, no evidence of violence, no evidence of chemical intervention. By every conventional metric, Professor Lionel Ashcroft had died of nothing at all.

But Lena Marchetti did not believe in nothing. She believed that whatever had happened in this room had been spoken.

She looked at the carved line one final time.

When breath becomes command, the body obeys.

Then she looked at the dead man's open mouth, his relaxed throat, his expression of profound and unmistakable relief.

"I want full audio from this building," she said. "Security mics, smart devices, HVAC systems, anything that records ambient sound. I want it all."

Kline raised an eyebrow. "You think someone talked him to death?"

Lena didn't answer the question. Not directly. Not yet. The shape of the thing was still forming in her mind, and she'd learned long ago not to speak a theory aloud before it could support its own weight.

Instead she said: "I think something happened in this room that didn't leave the kind of evidence we're trained to look for."

She turned toward the door, and as she did, her gaze swept one last time across the desk, the body, the walls of books, the undisturbed air, the whole composed, impeccable, impossible scene.

A room that had not fought back.

A man who had not struggled.

And a sentence carved into wood with the careful hand of someone who had wanted very much to be understood.

She was almost through the doorway when Kline spoke again.

"Lena. One more thing." He held up an evidence bag, clear plastic crinkling under the fluorescent hall light. Inside was a single sheet of paper, dense with handwritten text, corrections layered over corrections in an increasingly urgent hand. At the top, barely visible beneath the newer ink, was a title she couldn't quite make out from this distance.

"Found it in the printer tray," Kline said. "Fresh. Like he'd just pulled it."

Lena took the bag and held it up to the light.

The handwriting was Ashcroft's, she recognized the cramped, ascending style from the annotations in his books. But the text wasn't notes. It wasn't analysis. It was something else, lines arranged in a specific pattern, with deliberate spacing, structured in a way that looked less like academic notation and more like verse.

At the top, in a hand steadier than the rest, as though this part had been written first and with absolute certainty:

155

Just the number.

No title. No attribution.

Just three digits that meant nothing to most people alive and, Lena suspected, had meant everything to the man sitting dead in the room behind her.

She stared at it for a long moment.

"Bag it separately," she said, handing it back to Kline. "And get me everything you can find on what Ashcroft was researching. Every note, every file, every correspondence. I want to know what he found."

"What he found?" Kline repeated. "Or what found him?"

Lena looked at him.

For a moment, the hallway between them felt longer than it was, the fluorescent light thinner, the silence heavier, the distance between what she knew and what she suspected wider than any evidence could bridge.

"Both," she said.

And walked into the night.

• • •

CHAPTER TWO: *The Sound That Stayed*

The evidence lab had no personality, and Lena appreciated that about it. Clean data. Clear surfaces. No ambiguity. She needed that now, because the carved line from Ashcroft's desk was still reverberating inside her skull, and the strange, insistent way it had settled into her attention refused to fade.

When breath becomes command, the body obeys.

She had never encountered a sentence that felt like it was still working on her after she'd stopped reading it.

"Got the audio," Kline said, appearing beside her with a laptop and a pair of over-ear headphones that looked like they'd survived at least one divorce and possibly a war. "Building security had hallway cameras with built-in mics. No video or audio inside Ashcroft's office, he made sure of that, but the mic picked up some bleed when the door cracked open at various points during the evening."

"Quality?"

"Not great. Compressed. Lots of interference. But there's something on it." He set the laptop on the table and angled it toward her. The screen showed a waveform, jagged, noisy, the kind of visual that looked like a city skyline designed by an earthquake. "Timestamp lines up with the estimated window for time of death."

Lena took the headphones and placed them over her ears. The world outside, Kline's breathing, the hum of the lab, the distant murmur of the precinct, collapsed into silence. She adjusted the fit, letting the cups seal fully, creating the kind of acoustic isolation her work demanded.

"Play it," she said.

Kline tapped the spacebar.

Static filled her ears first, thin, brittle, like tissue paper being crumpled at the bottom of a well. Underneath it, the ambient sounds of a university hallway after hours: the tick of a heating system, footsteps at a great distance, the subliminal drone of building infrastructure doing its work in the dark.

Then... a voice.

Low. Male. Not loud enough to resolve into clear speech but not random either. It emerged from the static the way a figure emerges from fog: shape first, then detail, then the unsettling recognition that it had been there longer than you'd realized.

Lena didn't try to make out the words. Not yet. That was the mistake most people made when analyzing audio, they chased meaning before structure, tried to decode the message before understanding the medium. She listened instead for what her training had taught her to prioritize: cadence. The spacing between vocal events. The duration of pauses. The rhythm.

The voice moved in deliberate intervals.

Not conversational. Not the natural, irregular cadence of someone talking to themselves or leaving a voicemail or arguing on the phone. This was measured. Each vocal event occupied a specific space in time, followed by a pause that was neither too long nor too short, calibrated, she realized, to create a particular kind of expectation. The brain, hearing a pattern of sound-silence-sound-silence, naturally began predicting when the next sound would arrive. And when that prediction was met, when the voice returned exactly when the listener's neurology expected it to, something happened.

A micro-release. A tiny neurochemical reward for correct anticipation. Barely perceptible. But cumulative.

Through the distortion, a fragment resolved: "...breath... becomes..."

A pause. Measured. Exact.

"...command..."

Her chest expanded, not because she'd chosen to inhale, but because the spacing of the words had synchronized with her respiratory cycle without her permission. Two repetitions. That was all it had taken for the cadence to reach for her breathing and begin to pull it into alignment.

Lena tightened her diaphragm deliberately, forcing an exhale that broke the alignment.

"...the body..."

The audio stuttered. Distortion swallowed the rest.

The recording cut.

Silence rushed back in, filling the headphones with the hollow, pressurized quiet of a sealed space. Lena sat with it for a moment, letting her breathing return to its own native rhythm, irregular, autonomous, hers.

"Well?" Kline asked when she removed the headphones.

"Play it again."

He raised an eyebrow but didn't argue. She put the headphones back on, and this time she closed her eyes, not to immerse herself but to isolate the auditory channel from the visual. Without the distraction of the waveform, without the flickering of the lab's fluorescent lights, she could focus entirely on the temporal structure of what she was hearing.

The voice returned. The static parted for it like a curtain.

"...breath... becomes..."

She counted the intervals this time. Mapped them against her own heartbeat. Noted the precise duration of each pause and compared it to the standard relaxation breathing rate of twelve to sixteen cycles per minute.

The pauses matched.

Not approximately. Not within a comfortable margin of error. *Precisely*. The spacing between vocal events had been calibrated to the average human respiratory rhythm at rest, which meant that anyone listening in a relaxed state would find their breathing automatically synchronizing with the speaker's cadence. And once breathing was synchronized, the cascade was predictable: heart rate followed breathing, parasympathetic activation followed heart rate, suggestibility followed parasympathetic activation.

"...command..."

The word landed in the space between her exhale and her next inhale, the transition point, the moment of maximum neurological receptivity, when the body was neither full nor empty and the mind was, for a fraction of a second, open.

She felt it. A warmth in her sternum that had no physical source. A softening in the muscles of her shoulders that she had not authorized. The beginning of something that might have been compliance if she'd let it continue for another two seconds.

She ripped the headphones off.

Kline stared at her. "You look like you just touched a live wire."

"I'm fine." She set the headphones on the table with more care than they required. "The voice on that recording, it's not random speech. The cadence is engineered. The timing between words is calibrated to the human breathing cycle. Whoever was speaking in that room was using rhythmic entrainment to influence the listener's physiological state."

Kline processed that with the expression of a man who'd just been told his car engine was actually a very sophisticated clock. "In English?"

"Someone was using their voice to control Ashcroft's body."

A beat of silence.

"Okay," Kline said. "That's the weirdest thing I've heard this month, and I once had a suspect claim diplomatic immunity from Neptune." He leaned against the table. "So what, we're looking for someone with a really good radio voice?"

"We're looking for someone with an understanding of neurolinguistic rhythm that exceeds anything in the published literature," Lena said. "This isn't hypnosis. It's not persuasion. It's something more precise."

Kline studied her for a moment. "And the part where your breathing changed while you were listening?"

She met his eyes. She hadn't realized he'd noticed.

"Noted and corrected," she said.

"Mm-hmm." He didn't look reassured. "Let's go talk to the kid."

• • •

Harris Cole did not look like someone who had discovered a body.

That was the second thing that bothered Lena.

She watched him through the observation glass for a full thirty seconds before entering the conference room, studying not his words, he wasn't speaking, but his body. He sat upright in a plastic chair with his hands folded neatly in his lap, shoulders squared, posture precise. His eyes were clear, focused on the middle distance with the kind of studied neutrality that Lena associated with people who had been trained to present themselves well in stressful situations, or people who were working very hard to maintain a specific internal state.

Shock was messy. It leaked through the body in uncontrolled micro-expressions, postural collapses, respiratory irregularities. People in genuine shock fidgeted, or they froze in ways that looked frozen, rigid, brittle, ready to shatter. They did not sit in conference room chairs with the composed stillness of someone waiting for a job interview.

"Too calm?" Kline murmured beside her.

"Too organized," Lena said. "That's not shock. That's compensation."

"You think he's hiding something?"

"I think he's holding something together, and he may not know what it is."

She pushed the door open and stepped inside.

Harris looked up immediately. Early twenties. Clean-shaven, dark-eyed, with the slightly malnourished look of a graduate student who lived on coffee and departmental funding. His expression was attentive but blank, a face that had been carefully emptied of everything that might betray its contents.

"Mr. Cole," Lena said, taking the chair across from him. "I'm Dr. Lena Marchetti. I consult with the department on cases involving verbal evidence and communication analysis."

"I already told the detective everything I know," Harris said. His voice was steady. Even. No spikes, no dips. Almost rehearsed.

"I know you did. We're just going to go through it once more. Sometimes details surface on the second pass." She placed a small recorder on the table but didn't turn it on. She wanted the baseline first, his natural cadence, his breathing when he wasn't thinking about it. "Start from when you arrived at the building."

Harris swallowed, a small gesture that served as the sentence's period. "I came by around ten. Professor Ashcroft had asked me to drop off revisions for a chapter he was working on. He'd been working late all week. The door was unlocked when I got there, which was unusual, he usually kept it locked."

"Did you knock?"

"Yes. No answer. So I went in."

"And?"

A pause. It was the first break in his fluency, and Lena noted its duration: one point four seconds. Longer than a natural conversational pause, shorter than a deliberate stall. It was the kind of gap that appeared when someone was deciding, not what to say, but how much of what they remembered to include.

"I saw him sitting at the desk," Harris said. "I thought he was asleep at first. Then I noticed his eyes were open, and I called campus security."

"Before you called, what did you notice about the room?"

"Nothing unusual. It looked the way it always does."

"The carving on the desk?"

Harris's gaze dropped for a fraction of a second. A microexpression, not guilt, not evasion, but something closer to flinching. As though the mention of the carving had triggered a physical response he'd tried to suppress.

"I saw it," he said. "But I didn't really read it."

"Words carved into a desk, and you didn't read them?"

"I mean, I noticed them, but I didn't focus on them. I was more concerned with the fact that my advisor was dead."

Reasonable. Logical. The kind of answer that would satisfy most investigators and be accepted without further scrutiny.

But Lena wasn't most investigators.

"Say the line," she said.

Harris blinked. "What?"

"The line carved into the desk. You saw it. Say it."

Something shifted behind his eyes, a flicker of resistance, or recognition, or both. His hands tightened slightly in his lap.

"I don't remember it exactly."

"You don't need to remember it exactly. Just say what you recall."

His lips parted. Closed. Parted again.

"When... breath... becomes..." he started, and Lena watched his breathing change in real time. The words reshaped his respiratory pattern as he spoke them, his chest rising in a slow, involuntary alignment with the rhythm of the syllables. Not dramatically. Not obviously. But measurably, to someone who knew what to look for.

He stopped.

Something flickered across his face. Not confusion. Recognition. The look of someone encountering a familiar sensation they hadn't expected to feel.

"...command," he finished, quieter.

The room shifted. Not physically, the walls didn't move, the light didn't change, the air didn't thicken. But perceptibly. As though something that had been dormant in the space between them had been given permission to wake up.

Kline shifted against the wall. Lena felt him tense, though she didn't look.

Harris's breathing had changed. Deeper now. Slower. His shoulders, which had been locked in that precise, compensatory posture since she'd entered the room, softened by a degree. His eyes, still focused on her, had lost a fraction of their sharpness, not unfocused, but less defended. As though the act of speaking those words had opened a valve somewhere inside him that he hadn't known was closed.

"Continue," Lena said gently.

Harris swallowed. "The body..."

The phrase lingered. Unfinished. Waiting.

And then, so softly that Kline might have missed it if the room hadn't been absolutely silent, Harris whispered a word that completed the sentence.

"...obeys."

Lena's pulse ticked once, hard, against the inside of her wrist.

That word had not been in the audio recording.

The recording had cut out after "the body." The rest had been swallowed by distortion. Whatever had followed that fragment, whether it was the word Harris had just spoken or something else entirely, had not been captured, had not been transcribed, and had not been shared with Harris Cole at any point during his interview or the investigation.

He had no way of knowing how that sentence ended.

"Stop," Lena said, sharper than she intended.

Harris blinked hard, the way people do when surfacing from water, a full-body reset, consciousness re-engaging with the room around him as though it had briefly gone somewhere else.

"What?" he said. "I didn't, what was I saying?"

"You completed the phrase."

Harris shook his head. "No, I was just repeating the line from the desk."

"The line from the desk ends with *the body obeys*. You said 'when breath becomes command', and then you added the rest."

"That's... I must have read the whole thing."

"You told me you didn't focus on it."

Something cracked in Harris's composure, a hairline fracture running through the careful structure he'd built around himself. His fingers tightened against each other, and for the first time since she'd entered the room, his breathing was uneven. Irregular. Human.

"I don't understand," he said, and his voice cracked on the last word, the composure he'd been maintaining all interview finally splitting along a fault line he couldn't repair.

"Mr. Cole, did you hear anyone speaking when you entered Professor Ashcroft's office?"

He hesitated. Not the practiced, fluent hesitation of his earlier answers. A genuine pause. The kind that happened when the mind was sorting through something it didn't want to find.

"I... don't think so," he said.

Don't think. Not *no.* Not the clean, confident denial he'd given before.

"You told Detective Kline the room was quiet."

"It was quiet."

"But the hallway microphone picked up a voice."

Harris's head came up. "That's not possible. I was right there. I would have heard it."

"Unless," Lena said carefully, "you weren't listening."

"I was listening." The insistence was immediate and brittle.

"You were present," Lena corrected. "That's not the same thing."

Silence fell between them. The kind of silence that had weight and texture and an agenda of its own. Harris shifted in his chair, the first truly uncontrolled movement he'd made since she'd been watching him, and something in his face changed. The careful blankness dissolved, and what remained underneath it was not guilt or evasion or composure but something rawer and more honest.

Fear.

Not of Lena. Not of the investigation.

Of whatever was sitting quietly in the back of his mind, repeating itself in a rhythm he couldn't quite hear and couldn't quite forget.

"I think," Lena said, "you heard something in that room. And I think your mind decided not to keep it."

Harris's lips parted. No words came out. But his chest rose, just slightly, just once, out of rhythm.

And that involuntary breath told Lena Marchetti everything she needed to hear.

• • •

CHAPTER THREE: *The Hand That Wrote Before*

Professor Lionel Ashcroft had not been a disorganized man.

That much was immediately clear from the evidence archive, where every item from his office had been laid out across two stainless steel tables in the order it had been collected, tagged, and sealed. The arrangement was meticulous, books grouped by subject and shelving location, papers stacked in the order they'd been found, personal effects bagged separately and placed at the far end of the second table like afterthoughts that hadn't earned their place among the work.

Lena stood at the head of the first table, latex gloves on, and surveyed the terrain. She'd arrived at seven in the morning, two hours before Kline was due, because she wanted time alone with Ashcroft's collection. Not for any mystical reason, she didn't believe in the vibrational residue of dead men or the psychic echoes of scholarly obsession, but because the kind of reading she needed to do was best done without conversation. Other people's voices were noise, and noise interfered with pattern recognition.

She started with the books.

The collection was substantial and narrow, the library of a man who had spent decades drilling into a single vein of inquiry. Early modern linguistics. Phonetic reconstruction. Prosody studies spanning three centuries. Several editions of Shakespeare's complete works, each annotated in different colors of ink that corresponded, Lena guessed, to different periods of Ashcroft's career. The earliest annotations were written in the careful, tentative hand of a young academic establishing his methodology. The later ones were tighter, faster, more urgent, the handwriting of a man who had stopped caring about penmanship because something else had become more important.

She moved down the line, noting titles, checking spines for wear patterns, filing observations. Most of the books were well-used but unremarkable, the standard toolkit of a historical linguist with a Shakespeare specialty. She was halfway down the second table when one volume made her stop.

It wasn't the title that caught her attention. It was the condition.

Shakespeare's Sonnets, 1609 Quarto (Reproduction Edition)

A facsimile of the Thomas Thorpe quarto, the kind of thing university libraries kept in their rare books rooms and professors ordered personal copies of when their research demanded constant access. But this copy had been handled far beyond the normal range of academic use.

The spine was softened almost to the point of collapse. The pages were slightly warped from pressure and repeated opening at specific locations. The cover bore the particular kind of wear that came from being carried, in bags, in hands, on trains, in beds, rather than simply shelved and consulted.

This book had been a companion. A project. A fixation.

Lena set it aside and continued to the papers.

Ashcroft's notes were a palimpsest of thought, ideas layered over ideas, revised, reconsidered, abandoned, resurrected. His process wasn't linear. It was iterative, circling the same questions with increasing precision, narrowing his focus the way a lens focused light until the point of concentration became hot enough to burn.

She found the page she was looking for near the middle of the second stack.

At the top, in Ashcroft's hand:

Cadence over Content

Below it, lines of verse had been transcribed, fragments, not complete poems. Phrases pulled from various sources and rearranged not for meaning but for timing. Words repositioned not because they said something different in a new order, but because the new order changed the *spaces between them*, altered the rhythm in which a reader's eye, or a listener's ear, would encounter them.

He hadn't been studying what Shakespeare said. He'd been studying how Shakespeare *sounded.*

Lena turned the page.

What she found next made her set down the stack and pull the lamp closer.

Listener Response Variance, Subjective Reports

The heading was clinical. The content beneath it was anything but.

Subject 3: Reports warmth in chest. Reduced inclination to interrupt or disagree. Duration: approximately 4 minutes post-exposure.

Subject 7: Mild euphoria. Described as "a feeling of being held." Loss of resistance to conversational direction. Duration: 6-8 minutes.

Subject 11: Distress. Rejection. Described experience as "invasive." No measurable compliance shift. Subject declined further participation.

Lena read the entries twice, her mind running calculations she didn't want to complete. These were not theoretical notes. These were observations from live experiments. Ashcroft had been testing something on human subjects, testing the effect of specific rhythmic patterns on emotional state, compliance, and physiological response.

"He was running experiments," she murmured to herself, and the word *experiments* felt insufficient for what the data implied.

She set the listener reports aside and reached for the next page in the stack.

It was different from the rest.

Not notes. Not analysis. Not the cramped, urgent handwriting of a researcher chasing an idea through revisions. This page had been written with deliberate care, each letter formed with the kind of attention that suggested the act of writing was itself significant, that the hand holding the pen understood it was transcribing something that mattered more than anything it had written before.

No corrections. No hesitation marks. No crossed-out words.

Just text.

Centered on the page.

And at the top, in a hand steadier than the rest:

155

Lena had seen this number before, on the page Kline had pulled from Ashcroft's printer tray the night before. But this was different. This was the source, or closer to it. The printer page had been a copy. This was the working document.

She leaned closer, and under the bright evidence lamp, she noticed something she'd missed at first glance. The ink was not uniform. Two different shades occupied the page, some lines darker, heavier, written with a newer pen. Others lighter, older, laid down at a different time with different pressure and different flow.

This page had been written in layers.

The darker lines, Ashcroft's recent work, filled in gaps, completed fragments, bridged sections where the lighter ink had been too faded or too incomplete to read. But the lighter lines were the foundation. They had been written first, and they had been written by someone else.

Or copied from someone else's work.

Lena read the first line.

When breath is lent to shape the yielding ear—

Her lungs adjusted.

The shift was immediate, involuntary, and precise. Not a gasp. Not a catch. A *recalibration*, her diaphragm moving to accommodate a breathing pattern that the words had suggested without her conscious participation.

The line's iambic rhythm mapped onto the natural expansion and contraction of the chest with the same quiet authority that a conductor's downbeat mapped onto an orchestra's first note. Her body had begun to follow before her mind had finished reading.

She stopped.

Closed her eyes.

Forced a sharp, irregular breath that broke the alignment the way you'd break a fall, with deliberate, graceless effort.

When she opened her eyes again, she didn't look at the page. She looked at the wall, at the sterile institutional blankness of it, and waited until her breathing was fully her own again.

"Don't read it straight through," she said quietly, to no one. A note to herself. A rule established in real time by a woman who had just learned something about herself that she did not want to examine too closely.

She turned to the quarto instead.

Gloves still on, she opened the reproduction carefully, turning pages with the controlled precision of someone handling something more dangerous than old paper. She wasn't reading. She was searching, scanning margins, checking blank spaces, looking for anything that didn't belong to the printed text.

Page after page passed. Shakespeare's sonnets marched by in their original typesetting, 154 poems in sequence, each one a self-contained universe of desire and mortality and the desperate hope that beauty could be preserved in language if the language was good enough. Lena knew them well, she'd studied them in graduate school, dissected their prosody in her dissertation research, taught them in a seminar she'd led for three semesters before leaving academia for consulting work that paid better and hurt differently.

She was eighty pages in when she found it.

Not the printed text.

The margin.

In the white space beside Sonnet 130, *My mistress' eyes are nothing like the sun*, a faint, almost invisible hand had written four lines of verse. The ink had faded to the color of weak tea, and the handwriting was not Ashcroft's. It was older in style, more ornate, with the kind of elaborate descenders and compressed spacing that suggested a hand trained in an earlier century's conventions.

The lines were not part of any published sonnet.

They were not numbered.

They were not attributed.

They were simply there, four lines of iambic pentameter tucked into a margin, waiting with the quiet patience of something that had been hidden in plain sight for a very long time.

Lena leaned in, angling the page under the evidence lamp to catch the faded ink at its most legible. She read the first line.

And felt it again.

Stronger this time. Not just a respiratory adjustment but a full-body resonance, a warmth in her sternum, a loosening in her shoulders, a subtle reduction in the baseline tension she carried in her jaw without ever being aware of it. The words settled into her nervous system like a key entering a lock: not forcing, not breaking, but finding the shape of an opening that was already there and filling it with a precision that felt less like reading and more like being *read*.

She snapped the book shut.

The sound was louder than she'd intended, a sharp crack of leather and paper that made the evidence technician at the far end of the room look up from his work.

"You okay?" Kline asked from the doorway. She hadn't heard him arrive, which meant she'd been more absorbed than she'd realized.

"Fine." She placed the book down slowly, keeping one gloved hand on its cover as though it might open itself if left unattended. "How long have you been standing there?"

"Long enough to watch you slam a book like it bit you." He crossed the room, coffee in hand, and leaned against the edge of the table. "What did you find?"

Lena looked at the closed quarto. At the page of layered ink with its number at the top. At the listener reports. At the trail of evidence that was beginning to arrange itself into a shape she recognized, not a random scatter of academic eccentricity, but a deliberate, decades-long research program aimed at a single, specific goal.

"Ashcroft wasn't creating something," she said.

Kline frowned. "He was studying something?"

"More than that." She tapped the quarto. "There's handwriting in this book that isn't his. It's older. Possibly much older. And the page with the fragments, it's written in two layers of ink. Ashcroft was filling in gaps."

"Gaps in what?"

Lena met his eyes. "In something that someone else started. Something that's been passed down, fragment by fragment, possibly for centuries."

Kline took a slow sip of his coffee. "So you're telling me our dead Shakespeare professor was working on some kind of... ancient poem?"

"Not just a poem. A *system*." She gestured to the listener response reports. "He was testing its effects on people. Documenting physiological responses. Classifying listeners by susceptibility."

"And this connects to his death how?"

"He had nearly finished reconstructing it. The page from the printer, the one labeled 155. It's almost complete. Whatever he'd been assembling from these fragments, he was close to having the whole thing."

Kline set his coffee down. "Okay. Back up. Shakespeare wrote 154 sonnets. Everybody knows that. You're saying there's a 155th?"

"I'm saying Ashcroft believed there was. And he believed it was deliberately left unpublished." She paused, choosing her next words with the care of someone laying a foundation that would need to support a great deal of weight. "I think the complete text was broken apart and distributed, hidden in margins, encoded in private correspondence, scattered across centuries, because whoever understood what it could do understood that a complete version was too dangerous to exist in one place."

Kline stared at her. "You're serious."

"When have I not been?"

"Fair point." He rubbed the back of his neck. "So we've got a dead professor, a mysterious ancient poem that makes people act weird, and now you're telling me this thing might be... what, historically significant?"

Lena didn't answer right away. She was looking at the quarto, at the sealed page of fragmented verse, at the whole carefully organized collection of a man who had spent his life following a trail of breadcrumbs that someone had laid down centuries ago.

Then she said: "I'm telling you that Ashcroft wasn't the first person to try to reconstruct this. And I'm telling you that the reason it was broken apart in the first place is the same reason Ashcroft is dead."

"Which is?"

Lena's gaze held steady, but something behind it shifted, a shadow of the sensation she'd felt when she'd read that first line. Not the sensation itself, which she'd broken cleanly and would not revisit. But the memory of it. The imprint. The knowledge that something in those words had reached past her training, past her expertise, past every defense she'd built in twelve years of studying manipulation, and had touched something underneath that she hadn't known was exposed.

"Because a complete version," she said, "would be too effective to control."

Kline let the silence hold for a moment. Then he picked up his coffee, took a long drink, and nodded once.

"I'm going to need a bigger whiteboard," he said.

• • •

CHAPTER FOUR: *The Invitation*

Lena kept her office the way other people kept their religions, with quiet devotion and no tolerance for heresy.

It occupied the third floor of a brownstone on West 113th Street, a short walk from Columbia's campus, where she maintained an adjunct affiliation that gave her library access and the occasional speaking invitation in exchange for lending the university her name on grant applications. The space was small, a converted bedroom in what had once been a faculty apartment, but she'd made it hers in the deliberate, exacting way she made everything hers: by removing whatever she didn't need and arranging what remained with the precision of a typesetter laying out a page.

Bookshelves on two walls, organized by methodology rather than subject. A desk facing the window, clean except for a laptop and a ceramic cup that held exactly four pens. No photographs. No plants. No decorative objects that might accumulate dust or sentiment. The only personal item in the room was a framed quote on the wall behind her chair, not inspirational, not literary, but clinical. A single line from a 1987 paper on coercive persuasion that she'd underlined in graduate school and never been able to forget:

The most effective manipulation is the kind that feels like your own idea.

Her ex-husband Marcus had hated that quote. He'd wanted her to take it down, said it made the office feel like a surveillance station, said it was morbid for a woman who should be focused on communication, not control. She'd kept it. He'd left. The causality was more complicated than that, of course, a marriage didn't end over a framed sentence, but the quote had outlasted the relationship, and Lena found a grim satisfaction in that fact that she tried not to examine too closely.

It was late afternoon when she returned from the evidence archive, her mind still sorting through the implications of what she'd found in Ashcroft's collection. She set her bag on the desk, opened her laptop, and began typing notes, not conclusions, not theories, but observations arranged in the order they'd occurred, because sequence mattered. The order in which you encountered information shaped the conclusions you drew from it, and Lena was careful to preserve the chronology of her own thinking the way a surveyor preserved the contour of the terrain.

She was forty minutes into her notes when the receptionist knocked.

"This came for you," she said, holding out an envelope. "Courier dropped it off about an hour ago. No return address."

Lena took it without comment and waited until the door closed before examining it.

Heavy stock. Cream, not white. The kind of paper that resisted folding, that preferred to remain intact, that announced its own quality without a letterhead or embossing. Her name was written on the front in precise, deliberate script, not calligraphy, not typeset, but *handwritten* with the confident spacing of someone who understood that the physical act of writing was itself a form of communication.

Dr. Lena Marchetti

No flourish. No title beyond the degree. Just accuracy.

She turned it over. No seal. No markings. No imperfections. Just the smooth, unblemished surface of paper that had been manufactured to a standard most people would never encounter and fewer would appreciate.

She opened it with her fingers, no letter opener, no ceremony. Inside was a single card, the same heavy stock as the envelope, bearing three lines of text:

You are asking the correct questions.

You are observing the correct patterns.

You are, however, proceeding too slowly.

Lena read the lines once, quickly, for content. Then she read them again, slowly, for structure.

The sentences were grammatically parallel, same subject, same progressive verb construction, same confident declarative tone. That was surface-level observation, obvious to anyone with a passing familiarity with rhetoric. What caught Lena's attention was underneath the grammar: the *cadence*. Each sentence was slightly longer than the last, adding one beat to the rhythm in a progression that created the subliminal impression of acceleration, of urgency gathering without ever being stated directly. The pauses between sentences, implied by the line breaks, were calibrated in the same way the voice on the hallway recording had been calibrated: long enough to create anticipation, short enough to maintain momentum.

Whoever had written this card understood the same principles she'd heard in that audio fragment. They weren't just communicating a message. They were communicating *in the medium itself*, embedding rhythm in prose, influence in syntax, control in the spaces between words.

She turned the card over.

Blank. No signature, no mark, no hidden text.

But when she angled it against the light from the window, tilting the card until the surface caught the low afternoon sun at exactly the right angle, she saw it. An embossing, pressed into the card stock with enough force to leave an impression but not enough to be visible under normal lighting.

Two words. Two numbers.

Tonight. Eight.

And beneath them, not an address but a phrase, three words that, to anyone else, would have looked like a fragment of poetry or an unfinished thought. To Lena, they looked like coordinates disguised as language.

She stared at them for a long time.

Then she picked up her phone and called Kline.

• • •

"This is a terrible idea," Kline said for the third time as they walked south on Amsterdam Avenue, the November air sharp enough to make his words visible.

"You said that already."

"I'm going for emphasis through repetition. I hear it's effective."

Lena smiled despite herself. "The card is an invitation. Refusing it tells them we're afraid. Accepting it on our own terms tells them we're not."

"And what are our terms, exactly? Because right now our terms appear to be 'walk into an unknown location at the request of an anonymous person who knows things they shouldn't know about an active murder investigation.'"

"Those are our terms, yes."

Kline muttered something about retirement that she chose not to hear.

She'd decoded the location in twenty minutes. The three words embossed beneath *Tonight. Eight.* weren't coordinates in the numerical sense, they were phonetic markers, stressed syllables that corresponded to a specific intersection when mapped against the rhythmic notation system used in historical prosody. It was the kind of code that would be invisible to anyone who didn't study the physical properties of speech for a living, which meant it was designed for her specifically.

That bothered her. But not enough to stay home.

The building was unremarkable in the way that only expensive things could be, so perfectly ordinary that its ordinariness became a kind of camouflage. A narrow stone facade between two larger, louder neighbors, its entrance unadorned, its windows dark, its only distinguishing feature a quality of maintenance that suggested someone cared very much about appearances and very little about being noticed.

No signage. No buzzer panel. No security camera.

Just a door.

Kline scanned the street with the practiced eye of a man who'd been in enough ambushes to know what the prelude looked like. "I don't love this."

"Noted." Lena reached for the handle.

The door was unlocked. Of course it was.

She pushed it open, and the city disappeared.

Not gradually. Not with the muffled transition of a well-insulated lobby. Completely. The sound of Amsterdam Avenue, traffic, voices, the low-frequency rumble of a subway passing beneath, cut off as though someone had pressed mute on the world. What replaced it was silence of a quality Lena had encountered only in professionally designed recording studios: not the absence of sound but the *control* of it. Active silence.

Engineered silence. Silence that had been built, at considerable expense, to be absolute.

The interior was minimal and precise. A narrow corridor, warmly lit from sources she couldn't identify, no visible fixtures, no overhead glare, just a diffuse amber glow that seemed to emanate from the walls themselves. The floor was polished concrete, the color of graphite. The air smelled faintly of cedarwood and something else she couldn't name, not a perfume, not an oil, but a note that existed at the edge of perception and pulled at the attention without offering itself for identification.

Kline's hand moved to his hip, where his holster sat beneath his jacket. Lena noticed but didn't comment. In his position, she'd have done the same.

They followed the corridor to its end, where it opened into a larger space, a room of deliberate proportions, wider than it was deep, with a ceiling high enough to create the acoustic profile of a small concert hall. The walls were paneled in dark wood. Two chairs faced each other in the center of the room, separated by approximately four feet of empty floor. Nothing else. No desk. No table. No art. No distraction.

A stage. That was what it was. A stage designed not for performance but for encounter.

And standing at the far end of the room, hands loosely at his sides, posture relaxed in a way that suggested not comfort but absolute command of his own body, was a man.

Lena's first impression was of precision. Not the cold, mechanical precision of a machine, but the warm, practiced precision of a musician, someone whose relationship with control was not rigid but *fluid,* who understood that true mastery looked like ease. He was lean, well-dressed in a way that communicated expense without announcing it, dark jacket, no tie, collar open, everything tailored to suggest that the body underneath made its own decisions about how to occupy space. Mid-forties or slightly older. Dark hair, touched with grey at the temples. A face that was handsome in the way that well-crafted objects were handsome: you noticed the quality of the construction before you noticed the aesthetics.

But it was his eyes that Lena registered most acutely. Dark. Attentive. Listening, not in the passive sense of receiving information, but in the active, focused sense of a man who had trained his perception to operate in registers that most people couldn't access. He looked at her the way she looked at crime scenes: with the patient, granular attention of someone who understood that the most important details were the ones that didn't announce themselves.

He inclined his head slightly as they approached.

"Dr. Voss," he said.

His voice was the first weapon she encountered.

Not because it was deep, or loud, or commanding in any theatrical sense. Because it was *placed*. Each syllable occupied a specific location in the acoustic space of the room, not thrown, not projected, but set down with the care of a jeweler setting stones. The consonants were clean. The vowels were open, resonant, carrying just enough warmth to create the impression of intimacy without crossing any line that would make a listener conscious of being influenced. And underneath the surface characteristics, the timbre, the register, the carefully modulated dynamics, there was a rhythm. Subtle. Almost imperceptible. But present, in the way that a pulse was present: constant, foundational, and easy to forget was there until someone drew your attention to it.

Lena noticed it immediately.

She also noticed that her breathing had shifted, just fractionally, just at the margins, to accommodate the spacing of his words. She corrected it before it could settle.

"Detective Kline," the man added, his gaze moving briefly to acknowledge Kline without surrendering focus.

Kline didn't respond. His jaw was tight, his posture squared, his body language communicating the universal police dialect for *I don't trust you and I want you to know it.*

Lena stepped forward. "You've been watching."

The man's expression didn't change, but something in the quality of his attention sharpened, a recognition, perhaps, that she was not going to begin with pleasantries or deference. Good. Neither was he.

"We've been waiting," he said.

"For what?"

"For you to arrive at the conclusions you're arriving at. You've done so more quickly than most."

"And the ones who didn't?"

A pause. Not dramatic. Calibrated. Long enough to create expectation, short enough to prevent doubt.

"They are no longer relevant," he said.

Kline took a half-step forward. "Okay, I've heard enough of the mysterious cryptic act. Who are you?"

The man turned his attention to Kline, and Lena watched the detective's body language undergo a subtle shift, not compliance, not submission, but a fractional reduction in aggression, as though the weight of the man's direct attention had applied a gentle downward pressure on Kline's confrontational energy. Kline noticed it too. She saw his jaw tighten further, compensating.

"My name is Julian Calder," the man said. "And I believe Dr. Voss has already begun to understand what we do."

"What you do," Kline repeated flatly. "And what is that?"

Julian's gaze returned to Lena. "You found the fragments."

It wasn't a question.

"Yes," Lena said.

"And you've heard the recording."

"Yes."

"And you felt it."

The room seemed to contract around that last sentence, not physically, not dramatically, but perceptibly. As though the space between them had been gently compressed by the weight of the acknowledgment Julian was asking for. He wasn't asking whether she'd observed an effect. He was asking whether she'd experienced one. Whether her body had responded. Whether the thing she studied for a living had, for the first time, studied her back.

Lena held his gaze. "I noticed a physiological response consistent with rhythmic entrainment. I corrected it."

Julian smiled. It was a small expression, contained and precise, and it didn't touch his eyes. "Of course you did."

A beat.

"Sonnet 155," Lena said. "That's what Ashcroft was reconstructing."

Julian inclined his head. "Though we don't use that name."

"What do you call it?"

Another pause. This one was different, not calibrated for effect but weighted with something that might have been respect, or caution, or the particular care that people took when speaking the names of things they considered sacred.

"The Instrument," he said.

Kline scoffed quietly. "The Instrument. Great. And you, what, play it?"

Julian's gaze didn't leave Lena's. "We have preserved it. Refined it. Studied its architecture and its effects. For a very long time."

"How long?" Lena asked.

"Long enough," Julian said, "that your Professor Ashcroft was not the first to attempt reconstruction. Nor the second. Nor the tenth."

The implication settled into the room like sediment, slowly, heavily, with the kind of permanence that resisted being swept away.

"You knew him," Lena said.

"We were aware of his work."

"Were you aware that he's dead?"

Julian's expression didn't change. But something behind it did, a ripple of something that might have been regret, or acknowledgment, or the controlled grief of a man who had anticipated a loss and chosen to absorb it privately rather than display it.

"Yes," he said.

"Did you kill him?"

The question landed without flourish. Lena delivered it the way she delivered all her important questions: flatly, without accusation, leaving the maximum possible space for the answer to reveal not just its content but its *shape*, the hesitations, the evasions, the micro-rhythms that separated truth from performance.

Julian held her gaze for a long, measured moment.

"No," he said. "But I may have made it possible."

Kline's hand twitched toward his hip. Lena raised a finger, barely, almost imperceptibly, and he stopped.

"Explain," she said.

Julian stepped to the side, not toward them but laterally, creating a shift in the room's geometry that redistributed attention without demanding it. A conductor's gesture, subtle, practiced, and entirely in command.

"The Instrument requires precision," he said. "Ashcroft understood the text, but he lacked the training to deliver it. He was a scholar, not a practitioner. He tried to perform what he'd reconstructed, and the result was..." He paused, and for the first time, Lena heard something in his voice that wasn't control. "Imprecise."

"Imprecise enough to kill him?"

"Imprecise enough to destabilize. The body's response to malformed cadence is not compliance, it is chaos. Cardiac arrhythmia. Neurological disruption. Seizure." He met her eyes. "He played with fire. Badly. And fire does not distinguish between the careful and the careless."

Lena filed that explanation, noted its internal consistency, flagged the places where it could be tested, and moved on.

"Why contact me?" she asked.

Julian studied her for a moment, and in that moment Lena felt the full weight of his attention, not as pressure, not as intrusion, but as *recognition*. The sensation of being seen by someone who understood exactly what they were seeing and had been looking for it for a long time.

"Because you are the first person in twenty years," he said, "who heard the recording and broke the pattern before it completed."

The room held still.

"That," Julian Calder said softly, "is very, very rare."

He turned slightly, gesturing toward the two chairs that faced each other in the center of the room.

"Sit," he said. "There is a great deal you need to understand, and I would prefer to explain it before anyone else dies."

Kline looked at Lena. She could read the question in his posture, *do we stay or do we leave, and if you say stay I'm going to remind you of this moment every day for the rest of our professional relationship.*

Lena looked at Julian. At the room he'd built. At the careful, terrifying elegance of everything he'd arranged.

And sat down.

• • •

CHAPTER FIVE: *The Performance*

Julian did not begin immediately, and Lena understood that the delay was itself a technique.

He stood near the center of the room with the unhurried ease of a man who had occupied this space so many times that it had begun to feel like an extension of his body. His hands were loose at his sides. His weight was centered, balanced, ready without appearing prepared. He looked like someone waiting for a piece of music to begin, not in the audience but at the instrument, in that charged, intimate moment between silence and the first note, when the musician's body already knew what was coming and the room did not.

Lena sat in the chair he'd offered, her posture deliberately asymmetric, right foot slightly forward, left shoulder angled back, weight distributed unevenly. Asymmetry disrupted entrainment. She'd learned that from her own research, and she deployed it now as unconsciously as a swimmer deployed buoyancy: not thinking about it, just trusting the principle.

Kline stood against the wall to her left, arms crossed, radiating skepticism the way a radiator radiated heat, consistently, indiscriminately, and without any obvious off switch.

"What I'm about to show you," Julian said, "requires a participant."

"Not me," Kline said immediately.

Julian's gaze didn't waver from Lena. "No. Not you."

A door opened at the far end of the room, one Lena hadn't noticed, set flush with the wood paneling and distinguished only by the faintest seam in the surface. A woman stepped through.

She was in her mid-thirties, dark-haired, with the kind of self-possessed beauty that came from knowing exactly how much space you occupied and choosing to occupy it deliberately. She wore a simple black dress that moved like water when she walked. No jewelry. No visible tension in her posture. She crossed the room to the second chair and sat down facing Julian with the relaxed familiarity of someone performing a routine, not bored, not anxious, but prepared in the way that regular swimmers are prepared for water.

"This is a volunteer?" Lena asked.

"A participant," Julian corrected gently. "She has done this before. She understands what will occur."

"Does she understand that she's being observed by a murder investigation?"

Julian's expression shifted, a subtle acknowledgment, the kind of look a teacher might give a student who'd asked a sharper question than expected. "She understands that you need to see this."

The woman looked at Lena. Her eyes were calm, open, and entirely present. Whatever she was about to experience, she was approaching it with the clarity of informed consent. That much, at least, was legible in her body language.

Kline muttered something that Lena didn't catch and probably wasn't meant to.

"Watch her breathing," Julian said. The instruction was directed at Lena. "Not her face. Not her words. Her breathing."

Lena shifted her attention to the woman's chest, tracking the rise and fall of her ribcage with the practiced precision of someone who had spent years learning to read the body's involuntary language. At rest, the woman was breathing at approximately fourteen cycles per minute, normal, relaxed, unremarkable. Her shoulders were down. Her jaw was loose. Baseline established.

Julian turned to face the woman.

And spoke.

"When breath is lent..."

The first three words fell into the room like stones dropped into still water. Not loud. Not forceful. Not accompanied by any of the theatrical trappings that Lena had half-expected, no dramatic pause, no leaning forward, no intense eye contact. Just three words, spoken in a voice that was barely louder than conversation, with a spacing between them that felt as natural and inevitable as the gap between heartbeats.

"...to shape the yielding ear..."

The woman's chest rose. Not dramatically. Not visibly, to someone who wasn't watching for it. But measurably, her inhale lengthened by approximately half a second, drawn just slightly beyond her natural rhythm by the cadence of Julian's delivery. Her diaphragm expanded more fully than it had at baseline, as though the words had created space inside her that needed to be filled.

Lena recognized the technique. She'd studied it. She'd written about it. She'd identified it in cult leaders' speeches, in corporate motivational addresses, in the particular vocal patterns of her ex-husband when he'd wanted something from her and was being too careful to ask directly.

But she had never seen it executed with this level of precision. The difference between what she'd studied and what she was witnessing was the difference between a textbook diagram of a wave and the ocean.

"...and cadence binds what reason would defy..."

The woman's breathing synchronized.

It happened on the third line, the point at which, Lena knew, rhythmic entrainment typically locked in. The body, having received two consecutive intervals that matched its own respiratory frequency, committed to the pattern on the third repetition, adjusting its internal rhythm to match the external stimulus with the same automatic efficiency that a heartbeat adjusted to a pacemaker's signal.

The woman's inhales now coincided precisely with Julian's pauses. Her exhales coincided with his words. They were breathing in tandem, not because she had chosen to, not because she was aware of it, but because the ancient, subcortical machinery that regulated her autonomic nervous system had accepted Julian's cadence as its new clock.

"...the pulse forgets the boundary of fear..."

The woman's shoulders dropped. A fraction of an inch. But Lena saw it, the involuntary release of the trapezius muscles that occurred when the sympathetic nervous system began to stand down, when the body's fight-or-flight architecture received a signal that said *safe, ease, relent.* It was the same muscular signature that Lena had seen in ASMR research, in deep meditation studies, in the physiological profiles of subjects under clinical hypnosis.

"...and learns at last the sweetness of comply."

The final word settled into the room and did not leave.

Lena felt it.

Not the meaning, she could hold meaning at arm's length, could analyze it without absorbing it the way a chemist could analyze a compound without tasting it. What she felt was the *structure*. The way the sentence resolved. The way "comply" landed on a stressed syllable after a sequence of unstressed ones, creating a rhythmic resolution that the listener's neurology experienced as completion, as satisfaction, as a tiny, private reward for having followed the pattern this far.

Her own breathing had shifted. She corrected it and moved on.

Julian continued without acknowledging the correction, though Lena was certain he'd noticed it. His attention remained on the woman, who was now breathing in perfect synchronization with his delivery, her posture softening by progressive degrees, her expression settling into something that Lena could only describe as *open*. Not blank. Not passive. Not the slack-faced vacancy of unconsciousness. More like the face of someone listening to music they loved, present, engaged, receptive, and entirely unbothered by the fact that they had stopped controlling what their body was doing.

"Let not the tongue declare what mind resists..."

The woman's lips parted. Slightly. A millimeter of space between them that hadn't been there before, the oral aperture relaxing in a way that signaled not speech but *receptivity*, the mouth assuming the posture of someone prepared to receive something rather than produce it. It was an intimate detail, and Lena felt a flush of discomfort at noticing it, the kind of discomfort that came from watching something private happen in plain sight.

"...for softer chains are forged in tempered sound..."

The word *chains* should have been alarming. In any other context, in a courtroom, in a therapy session, in the clinical literature on coercive control, the metaphor of chains would have triggered defensive processing, resistancc, rcjcction. But Julian's delivery folded the word into the cadence so seamlessly that it arrived not as a threat but as a promise. A promise of something the listener wanted, offered in a voice that made wanting feel like wisdom.

Lena's sternum warmed. She suppressed it, a deliberate, clinical correction, and returned her attention to the room.

Kline, beside her, stood unchanged. Arms crossed, posture rigid, breathing irregular and entirely his own. He was unaffected. Completely. Whatever the sonnet was doing to the woman in the chair and to the margins of Lena's composure, it slid off Kline like water off stone.

The woman, by contrast, had entered a state that Lena recognized from the clinical literature on deep relaxation but had never witnessed in a non-clinical context. Her breathing was slow and perfectly regular. Her muscle tone had reduced to the minimum necessary to maintain her seated posture. Her pupils were dilated, her skin slightly flushed, and her hands, which had been resting in her lap, had opened, palms up, fingers relaxed, in the universal posture of surrender.

Julian spoke the final lines.

"So speak me slow, and let resistance part—"

A pause. The longest one. Precisely calibrated to create maximum anticipation, to stretch the elastic of expectation to its breaking point without actually breaking it, so that when the final word arrived it would land with the accumulated force of everything the listener had been waiting for.

"—for I am not thy voice... but now thy heart."

The woman exhaled.

Long. Deep. Complete. An exhale that seemed to empty not just her lungs but her entire architecture of resistance, every held breath, every clenched muscle, every defended boundary she'd brought into the room with her. It was the most intimate sound Lena had ever heard in a professional context: the audible signature of a human being letting go of the last thing they'd been holding on to.

The silence that followed was not empty. It was *full*. Charged with the specific density of a completed act, the way a concert hall felt in the moment after the last note, when the music had ended but the audience's nervous systems hadn't yet realized it.

The woman sat motionless. Breathing. Slow and even and perfectly regulated. Her eyes were open but unfocused, her expression serene in a way that went beyond relaxation into something Lena didn't have a clinical term for. She looked like someone who had arrived somewhere she'd been trying to reach for a long time and was in no hurry to leave.

"Hey," Kline said. His voice was flat, practical, and aimed at the woman. "Hey, can you hear me?"

No response.

"She can hear you," Julian said calmly. "She is simply not interested in responding."

Kline's jaw tightened. "That's not how that works."

"It is how this works."

Julian raised a single finger, not commanding, not sharp, just a small, precise gesture, and the woman inhaled. A new breath, different from the ones before it. Voluntary. Awake. Her posture began to reassemble itself in a slow, deliberate progression, like a building being reconstructed from the foundation up. Her eyes refocused. Her hands closed. Her shoulders lifted.

She blinked. Looked around the room with the mild confusion of someone who had dozed off in a familiar chair and was surprised to find visitors.

"Was I—" she started.

Then stopped.

"I don't remember all of it," she said.

Julian stepped back, restoring the neutral distance between performer and participant. "It is rarely remembered in detail."

Kline moved toward her. "Are you okay? Do you need medical attention?"

The woman looked at him with an expression that managed to be both reassuring and slightly amused, as though he'd asked whether she needed a doctor after a massage.

"I'm fine," she said. "Better than fine, actually." She paused, searching for the right word the way you searched for the title of a song you'd just heard. "Clear."

She stood, smoothed her dress with an unconscious gesture, nodded once to Julian, and left through the same invisible door she'd entered.

The room held the shape of what had just happened for several seconds, the residual charge of an event that had been too precise and too strange to dissipate immediately.

Kline spoke first. "What did you do to her?"

Julian turned to him with an expression of patient curiosity. "I spoke to her."

"That wasn't speaking. That was—" Kline stopped, frustrated by the inadequacy of his vocabulary for what he'd witnessed. He looked at Lena. "Help me out here."

Lena was quiet for a moment. Not because she lacked words but because the words she had were competing with something else, a residual sensation in her chest that she'd been managing since the second line of the sonnet. A warmth. A pull. The ghost of a rhythm that her body had wanted to follow and her mind had refused to permit.

"It's neurolinguistic entrainment," she said, and her voice was steady, clinical, completely under control.

"Rhythmic vocal patterns synchronized to the listener's respiratory and cardiac cycles, creating a progressive parasympathetic cascade that reduces cognitive resistance and amplifies suggestibility."

"In English," Kline said.

"He used the rhythm of his voice to take control of her nervous system."

Julian smiled. "I wouldn't have said *take control.*"

"What would you have said?"

"I would have said I offered her body a rhythm it preferred to its own. And her body accepted." He turned to face Lena fully now, and the weight of his attention settled onto her with the warmth of a spotlight. "You felt it."

It was not a question. It was an observation made by someone who had been watching her as closely as she'd been watching the participant, and who had noticed every correction, every compensation, every micro-adjustment she'd made to keep herself outside the pattern.

"I noticed the entrainment mechanism engaging," Lena said carefully. "I disengaged."

"You resisted," Julian said. "There is a difference."

"Not one that matters."

"It matters enormously." He stepped closer, not into her space but toward the border of it, the way you approached a line you wanted someone to know you could see. "Disengagement implies separation. Resistance implies contact. You didn't separate from the pattern, Dr. Voss. You *fought* it. Which means it had already begun to work."

Lena held his gaze and said nothing, because he was right, and acknowledging it aloud would give the observation more weight than she was willing to let it carry.

"The participant was willing," she said instead, redirecting. "She knew what to expect. She came prepared to surrender. How much of what we just saw was the sonnet, and how much was her own anticipation?"

"An excellent question," Julian said, and the warmth in his voice told her he meant it. "The answer is: both. The Instrument amplifies what is already present. A willing listener responds more quickly and more deeply than an unwilling one. But willingness is not a prerequisite. It is an accelerant."

"And unwilling listeners?"

"Respond more slowly. Resist longer. But the cadence is patient, and the body is, ultimately, cooperative." His eyes held hers. "Most bodies."

"Not all."

"No. Not all." He glanced briefly at Kline, who was leaning against the wall with the expression of a man who had just watched a magic trick and was annoyed that he couldn't figure out how it was done. "Some minds are naturally irregular. They break pattern instinctively. They are, for our purposes, unreachable."

"And me?" Lena asked. The question surprised her, not because she didn't want to know the answer, but because she hadn't intended to ask it. It had emerged from somewhere beneath her professional composure, from the part of her that had felt the warmth in her sternum and wanted to understand it.

Julian studied her for a long, careful moment.

"You," he said, "are something I have not encountered before."

"Which is?"

"Someone who feels the pattern fully... and holds herself apart from it by force of will."

He paused, and the pause had the quality of a period at the end of a sentence that was not yet finished, a held note, a breath before the resolution.

"That is extraordinarily rare, Dr. Voss. And I should tell you, as someone who has studied this for most of my adult life, that it is also temporary."

Lena felt the words land in her chest like a cold stone.

"What do you mean?"

Julian's expression was not unkind. But it was not reassuring either. It was the expression of a man delivering a diagnosis he wished he could soften but respected his patient too much to distort.

"Resistance is not immunity," he said. "The pattern is patient. And each time you hear it, even fragments, even echoes, the resistance becomes slightly less automatic. The correction you make takes slightly more effort. The body remembers what it felt, even when the mind decides to forget."

He took a step back, restoring the professional distance that his proximity had eroded.

"You broke the pattern tonight," he said. "Admirably. Precisely. With a discipline I genuinely respect."

Another pause. This one was a door, opening.

"But the more you hear it," Julian Calder said softly, "the easier it becomes to follow."

Lena stood. The chair moved behind her with a sound that was too loud for the room, a sharp, real, ungoverned noise that broke the acoustic spell of the space like a stone breaking the surface of still water.

"Thank you for the demonstration," she said. Her voice was steady. Her posture was controlled. Her breathing was her own.

But underneath all of that, underneath the training and the expertise and the twelve years of learning to read the body's involuntary language, something had shifted. Something small and warm and patient had settled into a place she couldn't reach with analysis and didn't know how to name.

She walked toward the door. Kline fell into step beside her, and his presence was a relief she wouldn't acknowledge.

"Dr. Voss," Julian said behind her.

She stopped. Did not turn.

"When you find yourself thinking about the line you almost completed in the evidence lab," he said, "don't be alarmed. That's not weakness."

He let the silence hold.

"That's just the sound of something learning your name."

Lena walked out into the November air, and for the first time since she'd entered the building, she let herself breathe however she wanted.

It took her three blocks to realize she was breathing in iambic pentameter.

• • •

CHAPTER SIX: *The Ones It Cannot Reach*

Sleep did not come, and Lena did not chase it.

She lay in her apartment on West 108th Street and replayed the moment on the walk home when she'd realized her breathing had settled into a rhythm she hadn't chosen. Five beats in, three beats held, five beats out. Iambic. She'd broken it immediately, forced an irregular pattern, held it for six blocks, let her body find its own cadence again.

But the fact that she'd had to reset at all was the thing she couldn't stop thinking about.

She had always believed that understanding the mechanism conferred immunity. That knowing how the trick worked made you undeceivable.

Marcus had taught her otherwise.

Marcus Wren. Ex-husband. Defense attorney whose courtroom voice she'd once described, in the privacy of her own assessment, as "architecturally manipulative." Three years of their marriage spent deploying the exact techniques she studied, cadence modulation, strategic pausing, embedded commands nestled in seemingly casual conversation. She hadn't noticed. The woman who studied verbal manipulation for a living had been verbally manipulated in her own kitchen, in her own bed, in conversations she'd thought were intimate and had later realized were *constructed*. When she'd finally seen it, during a dinner party, watching Marcus redirect a friend's objection with a vocal pattern she recognized from her own research, the recognition had been so sudden that she'd set down her wine glass and left the room without a word.

The marriage had ended two months later. The shame had lasted longer.

Understanding the mechanism did not confer immunity. It conferred *awareness*. And awareness without immunity was just a front-row seat to your own undoing.

She got out of bed. Put on coffee. Sat at her desk in the dark and did not open her laptop.

Instead, she thought about Julian's voice. Not what he'd said, what he'd *done* with the space between his words. The way each pause had been precisely long enough to create anticipation without allowing doubt. The way his vowels had resonated in a frequency range that she knew, from her own research, was associated with perceived authority and emotional safety. The way the whole performance had been simultaneously clinical and intimate, as though he were conducting surgery and making love with the same instrument at the same time.

She thought about the woman in the chair, and the expression on her face when the sonnet completed, and the word she'd used afterward: *clear*.

Not *good*. Not *relaxed*. Not *strange*.

Clear.

As though something that had been clouding her perception had been removed, and what remained was simpler and truer than what had been there before.

Lena drank her coffee and watched the sky lighten over Morningside Heights and made a decision that she recognized, even as she made it, as the kind of decision that separates the life you've been living from the life you're about to live.

She would go back. And she would ask Julian to do it to her.

• • •

Kline met her outside the building at four in the afternoon, which was the earliest Julian had agreed to receive them. The November light was already failing, the sky the color of pewter, the trees along Amsterdam Avenue reduced to black scaffolding against the grey.

"For the record," Kline said, "I think this is a bad idea."

"For the record," Lena said, "I'm aware."

"Also for the record, if something goes wrong in there, I'm pulling you out. I don't care if you're in the middle of a scientific breakthrough or a religious experience or whatever the hell this is going to be. You start acting like that woman last night, I'm stepping in."

"Agreed."

"You agreed too fast. That makes me nervous."

Lena looked at him. Kline stood in the cold with his hands in his coat pockets and his collar turned up against the wind, and despite the gruffness and the reflexive skepticism, there was a genuine concern in his face that she found both touching and slightly annoying. He didn't understand what she was doing. He didn't need to. He just needed to be there, being regular and irregular and fundamentally resistant to anything that tried to make him fall into line.

"You're my control variable," she said.

"I've been called worse."

They went inside.

Julian was waiting in the same room, standing in the same position, wearing the same unhurried composure, and yet something was different. Lena felt it before she could identify it: a subtle shift in the quality of his attention, the way a musician's focus changes when they move from rehearsal to performance. He'd been waiting for them, but he'd been waiting for *her*, and the distinction was legible in the way his eyes tracked her entrance, cataloguing her posture, her breathing, her emotional state with the granular precision of someone reading a text he'd been studying for a very long time.

"Dr. Voss," he said. "You've returned."

"I have a request."

Julian's eyebrow lifted fractionally. "I'm listening."

"Try it on me."

The room held its breath. Kline's body language tightened. Julian's did not, he remained perfectly still, perfectly composed, but Lena saw something move behind his eyes: interest. Genuine, acute, undisguised interest. The interest of a scientist presented with an anomalous result, or a chess player presented with a move they hadn't anticipated.

"You understand what you're asking," he said.

"I understand that I need to know how this affects someone who is actively resisting. I can't study a phenomenon I haven't experienced. And I can't resist effectively if I don't know what I'm resisting."

Kline stepped forward. "Lena—"

"I won't go under," she said, not looking at him. "I know the mechanism. I know the countermeasures. And I have you." She gestured toward him. "If my breathing synchronizes, if my posture changes, if I show any signs of entering a compliance state, you intervene."

"How?"

"However you want. Yell. Shake me. Throw cold water on my face. I don't care. Just break the pattern."

Kline looked at Julian with an expression that communicated, in the universal shorthand of men who carried badges, that if anything went wrong he would make Julian's life extremely complicated.

Julian ignored him. His attention was entirely on Lena, and the quality of that attention had shifted again, from professional curiosity to something more personal. He was looking at her the way he'd looked at the sonnet fragments in Ashcroft's notes: with the focused, almost reverent attention of someone who had found something rare and was deciding how carefully to handle it.

"Very well," he said.

Lena moved to the center of the room. She adjusted her stance deliberately, feet at uneven intervals, shoulders at different heights, weight shifted to one side. Maximum asymmetry. Maximum disruption potential. She controlled her breathing: irregular, unpredictable, deliberately varied in both depth and timing. No pattern for the entrainment to lock onto. A moving target.

Julian positioned himself four feet in front of her. Close enough for vocal resonance. Far enough for objectivity.

"Ready?" he asked.

"Proceed."

He began.

"When breath is lent..."

Lena inhaled sharply. Off-rhythm. Too fast. Breaking alignment before it could form.

"...to shape the yielding ear..."

She exhaled too soon, too hard, forcing her diaphragm into a pattern that contradicted the cadence of his words. The entrainment mechanism reached for her respiratory cycle and found nothing to grab, no regular rhythm, no predictable interval, no stable frequency to synchronize with.

"...and cadence binds..."

She shifted her weight. Right foot to left. Introducing a new variable, a physical disruption that further confused the body's tendency to settle into received patterns. Her shoulders moved out of alignment. Her jaw tightened on the left side, relaxed on the right. Every cell of her body was operating in deliberate, cultivated irregularity.

"...what reason would defy..."

Nothing. No pull. No warmth. No softening. The words slid past her like water off glass, present, audible, meaningful, but unable to find purchase on a nervous system that refused to hold still long enough to be caught.

Kline exhaled quietly behind her. She could feel his relief without seeing his face.

Julian's expression was composed, attentive, and, for the first time since she'd met him, genuinely impressed.

He continued.

"...let not the tongue..."

Something in his delivery shifted. The change was so subtle that Lena almost missed it, a fractional adjustment in timing, a slight modification to the length of the pause between phrases, a barely perceptible deepening of the resonant frequency of his voice. He was adapting. In real time. Reading her disruptions and adjusting his approach the way a jazz musician adjusted to an unexpected key change: not fighting it, not ignoring it, but *incorporating* it into the performance.

"...declare what mind resists..."

There. A flicker. Not a pull, not the full-body warmth she'd felt the night before, but a moment of alignment. A fraction of a second in which her breathing almost synchronized, in which her body's desire to fall into the offered pattern briefly overcame her deliberate irregularity. She felt it the way you felt a strong current brushing your ankles while standing in surf: not enough to move you, but enough to remind you that the water was capable of it.

She cut it. Hard. Sharp inhale, staggered exhale, asymmetric weight shift. The flicker died.

Julian's eyes narrowed, not with frustration but with the focused fascination of someone watching a phenomenon they'd theorized about but never observed.

"...for softer chains are forged in tempered sound..."

He stepped closer. Not dramatically. Half a step. But the reduction in distance changed the acoustic equation, his voice now had more chest resonance reaching her, more low-frequency vibration transmitted not just through the air but through the floor, through her bones, through the conducting medium of the body itself.

Another flicker. Stronger this time. Her breathing threatened to align for a full second before she wrested it back.

Julian stopped.

Mid-sequence. Mid-line. The cadence broke off cleanly, without resolution, leaving the pattern incomplete and the room filled with the charged silence of something that had been building toward a destination it would never reach.

He studied her.

Not with the professional detachment of a researcher. Not with the composed distance of a man accustomed to watching people surrender to his art. With something rawer and less controlled, the look of a person who had just encountered, in the midst of a landscape they knew intimately, a feature they had never seen before.

"Fascinating," he said. The word carried more weight than it should have. It sounded, in his mouth, less like an adjective and more like a confession.

Lena's breathing was ragged, not from the sonnet's effect but from the effort of resisting it. She'd been maintaining deliberate irregularity for nearly two minutes, which was cognitively exhausting in a way that most people never experienced. Voluntary control of the autonomic nervous system was possible but costly. It was like holding a door closed against a wind that never stopped pushing, you could do it, but not forever, and not without being aware of the force on the other side.

"You adapted your delivery," she said, steadying her voice.

"Of course." Julian's composure had returned, but something underneath it had changed, a new alertness, a new interest that hadn't been there before. "The standard cadence couldn't lock onto your breathing. So I adjusted."

"And it almost worked."

"Yes. Almost." He tilted his head, studying her with an attention that felt less like observation and more like touch. "You are not Resistant, Dr. Voss."

"I just resisted."

"No," he said gently. "You *fought*. There is a significant distinction." He clasped his hands behind his back, a settling gesture, the kind of movement a man made when he was about to say something he'd been thinking about for a while. "The people we classify as Resistant don't feel the pattern at all. Their neurological architecture simply doesn't engage with the stimulus. It's like color blindness, the signal arrives, but the receiver can't process it. They are safe. Permanently. Effortlessly."

He paused, letting the implications gather.

"You felt it. Both nights. You felt the warmth, the pull, the beginning of synchronization. Your body responded. It responded eagerly, if my observation serves. And then you stopped it, not because your neurology rejected the pattern, but because your *will* overrode your neurology."

Kline cleared his throat. "Is there a version of this where you stop analyzing her and start explaining what that means?"

Julian looked at him briefly, then back at Lena. "It means she is Receptive. Highly Receptive, in fact. Possibly one of the most Receptive individuals I've encountered. Her body wants to follow the pattern. Her mind refuses to let it."

He took a breath, and for just a moment, Lena thought she saw something in his eyes that was neither clinical nor strategic. Something closer to awe. Or longing. Or the particular sadness of a man who had spent his life perfecting an art he could never personally experience.

"That kind of resistance is extraordinary," he said. "It is also, I must be honest with you, finite."

Lena felt the words settle into her body like cold water. Not because she hadn't anticipated them, she had, in the dark of her apartment, in the hours between sleep and coffee. But because hearing them confirmed a truth she'd been managing since the evidence lab.

"Each exposure," she said.

"Yes," Julian replied. "Each exposure. Each fragment heard, each partial cadence encountered, each moment of alignment, even the ones you break, leaves a trace. The body remembers the pattern it was offered, even when the mind declines. Over time, the effort required to resist increases. The flickers become longer. The corrections become harder."

He held her gaze with an intimacy that had nothing to do with desire and everything to do with understanding.

"I've seen it happen before," he said. "To someone very like you. Brilliant. Disciplined. Aware of every mechanism at work. He resisted for months. He believed, as you do, that knowledge was sufficient protection."

The room contracted around the past tense.

"What happened to him?" Lena asked.

Julian's expression didn't change, but something behind it darkened, a shadow passing behind glass.

"He is alive," Julian said. "But I would not call what he does *living*."

Kline shifted against the wall. "Where is he?"

Julian held Lena's gaze for a moment longer, and in that moment she understood that he was deciding something, not whether to tell her, but how much of the truth she was ready to absorb.

"I would like to show you," he said. "If you're willing."

Lena looked at Kline. He looked back at her with an expression that said, clearly and without ambiguity, *I know you're going to say yes and I want you to know that I think it's a terrible idea and also I will be standing right next to you the entire time.*

She turned back to Julian.

"Show me."

• • •

The drive home was quiet.

Kline drove. Lena sat in the passenger seat, watching the city pass through rain-specked glass, the streetlights and storefronts blurring into a smear of color that her mind processed without engaging. They'd agreed to visit the person Julian had mentioned, tomorrow, in daylight, with backup aware of their location. Kline had insisted on the precautions, and Lena had agreed without argument, because the truth was that she was tired in a way that sleep wouldn't fix.

She thought about the flicker. The moment during Julian's delivery when her breathing had almost synchronized, when her body had leaned toward the offered pattern the way a plant leaned toward light, not choosing, not deciding, just *responding* to something it recognized as nourishment.

She thought about Marcus. About the three years she'd spent being expertly, lovingly managed by a man whose voice had been his primary instrument of control, and how she hadn't seen it until she'd seen it, and how the seeing had broken something inside her that she'd been rebuilding ever since.

She thought about Julian's eyes, and the particular quality of attention he'd directed at her during the test, not the professional interest of a researcher, but something more personal, more specific, the look of a man who had found something he'd been looking for without knowing he was looking.

She thought about the word *Receptive*, and what it meant that the most dangerous quality she could possess was the one she couldn't change.

Kline pulled up outside her building. The engine idled. Rain tapped against the roof with the random, unpattern-able rhythm of weather, nature's own resistance to entrainment.

"You okay?" he asked.

"Yes."

"That wasn't convincing."

"It wasn't meant to be." She opened the door, letting the cold air cut across her face. "I'm processing. It's what I do."

"Yeah, well, process with the doors locked and maybe a glass of wine."

She almost smiled. "Good night, Aaron."

"Good night, Lena. And for the record—" He waited until she looked at him. "You did good in there. Whatever he says about Receptive and resistance and all that. You didn't go under. That counts."

She held his gaze for a moment, letting the simple decency of the statement wash over her the way the rain was washing over the windshield, steady, natural, owed to nothing but gravity and kindness.

"Thank you," she said.

She closed the door. Walked up the steps. Let herself in. Locked the door behind her.

Stood in the dark hallway of her apartment, coat still on, keys still in her hand.

And noticed that she was humming.

A melody she didn't recognize. Not a song. Not a tune. Just a sequence of tones arranged in a pattern that her throat was producing without her conscious participation, a pattern that rose and fell in intervals she recognized, with a horrible, intimate clarity, as the rhythmic skeleton of the lines Julian had spoken.

She stopped.

The silence that followed was louder than the humming had been.

Lena set her keys on the hall table. Removed her coat. Walked to the bathroom. Ran cold water over her wrists until her pulse was her own again.

Then she looked at herself in the mirror and said, quietly, to no one but the woman looking back at her:

"It's already in you."

The woman in the mirror did not disagree.

• • •

CHAPTER SEVEN: *The One Who Broke*

The facility did not announce itself.

It occupied the second and third floors of a brownstone on a residential street in Murray Hill, indistinguishable from the private medical offices and discreet therapy practices that populated the neighborhood. No sign. No plaque. A single buzzer beside a door that Julian pressed without hesitation, as though he'd done it enough times to have stopped thinking about what waited on the other side.

They were admitted by a woman in clinical whites who nodded to Julian with the minimal courtesy of someone accustomed to visits that were neither social nor welcome. She led them up a narrow staircase, through a corridor that smelled of antiseptic and machine-filtered air, and stopped at a door marked only with a room number.

"How long?" Lena asked Julian as they walked. She'd been quiet since they'd left the performance space, not processing, exactly, but preparing. Building the professional distance she would need for whatever came next.

"Three years," Julian said.

Kline stopped walking. "Three *years*?"

Julian turned back. "Daniel Mercer was a researcher. A neurolinguist, like Dr. Voss, though less accomplished. He joined the Order voluntarily. He was fascinated by the mechanism and wanted to study it from the inside." A pause. "He was warned about the risks of extended exposure. He chose to continue."

"Chose," Kline repeated, investing the word with the particular flatness he reserved for things he considered bullshit.

"Yes," Julian said. "Chose. We do not compel participation. We never have."

"Just make it really hard to stop."

Julian didn't respond to that. Instead, he opened the door.

The room was small and clean, furnished with the deliberate minimalism of a space designed to manage a single patient with maximum efficiency and minimum stimulation. A hospital bed, angled slightly upright. A chair beside it, empty. Monitoring equipment, heart rate, respiration, EEG, displaying steady readouts in quiet green lines. A window, curtained. A floor, clean. Nothing extraneous. Nothing that could generate pattern or rhythm or the suggestion of either.

And in the bed, sitting upright with the precise, architectural stillness of a mannequin, was Daniel Mercer.

Lena had prepared herself for something dramatic, convulsions, restraints, the visible distress of a body fighting against its own malfunction. What she found was worse. Daniel was calm. His eyes were open, fixed on a point in the middle distance with an expression that was not blank but *occupied*, the face of someone listening intently to something that existed in a register no one else could hear. His posture was relaxed, his hands resting on the blanket with an unsettling symmetry, his body arranged in the careful, balanced stillness of a vessel that had been emptied of everything except the single function it was still performing.

His breathing was perfect.

Lena saw it immediately and felt the recognition settle into her stomach like a stone. Fourteen cycles per minute. Each inhale precisely measured. Each exhale precisely controlled. No variation. No irregularity. No deviation from the pattern, the same pattern she'd heard in the hallway audio, the same pattern Julian had deployed in the performance, the same pattern she'd felt reaching for her own diaphragm every time she encountered even a fragment of the sonnet's cadence.

Daniel Mercer was breathing in iambic pentameter.

"Jesus," Kline said quietly.

Lena moved closer. Slowly, the way you approached something that might be fragile or might be dangerous and you weren't yet sure which. The monitoring equipment tracked Daniel's vitals with the dispassionate consistency of machines that had long since stopped finding their patient's condition remarkable. Heart rate: 62 beats per minute. Respiratory rate: 14 cycles per minute. Oxygen saturation: 98 percent. By every metric the machines could measure, Daniel Mercer was in perfect health.

She stepped closer still, and that was when she saw it.

His lips were moving.

The movement was so subtle that from across the room it was invisible, a millimeter of displacement, repeated in a pattern so regular that it looked less like speech and more like the autonomous twitching of a muscle group that had locked into a loop. But this close, leaning over the bed rail with her face eighteen inches from his, Lena could read the shapes his lips were forming.

Words.

Spoken without sound.

Repeated without pause.

She watched his lips for ten seconds, tracking the cycle. The same sequence, over and over: a cluster of shapes that resolved, after three repetitions, into syllables she recognized.

...speak me slow... and let resistance part...

Lena's chest tightened. Not the warm, seductive tightening of entrainment, something colder, sharper. Recognition. Those were lines from the sonnet. Not the fragments she'd heard in the recording or seen carved into Ashcroft's desk. New lines. Lines she hadn't encountered yet.

So speak me slow, and let resistance part—

The rhythm of the words threaded through her ribcage before she could stop it, pulling at her breathing with the insistent gentleness of a hand on a leash. She felt her diaphragm begin to adjust, her respiratory cycle reaching toward the cadence that Daniel's silent lips were mapping in the air between them.

She stepped back.

Hard. Two steps. Three. Creating distance the way you created a firebreak, not enough to feel safe, but enough to stop the spread.

Kline was beside her. "What is it? What's he saying?"

"Lines from the sonnet," Lena said. Her voice was controlled, but she could hear the effort in it, the sound of someone speaking through a muscle that wanted to be doing something else. "He's repeating fragments. Continuously. Without input, without stimulus, without external reinforcement."

She looked at Julian, who stood near the door with his hands clasped behind his back and an expression that contained, beneath its composed surface, something that might have been grief.

"How is this possible?" she asked. "The sonnet requires delivery. Voice, cadence, proximity. Without ongoing stimulation, the effect should degrade."

"It does," Julian said. "In most cases. Responsive listeners recover within minutes. Even Receptive listeners return to baseline within hours." He looked at Daniel, and the look was the most human thing Lena had seen from him, not the calibrated attention of a performer or the focused interest of a scientist, but the unguarded sadness of a man looking at something he'd helped create and could not undo. "Daniel was exposed to the full sonnet, performed by a skilled practitioner, for three consecutive days. Twelve sessions. Approximately forty minutes each."

"Why?" Kline asked, and the word carried the weight of a man who was rapidly approaching the limits of what he could witness without arresting someone.

"Research," Julian said. "He wanted to map the full neurological cascade. He believed that extended exposure would allow him to observe the process from the inside, to experience it consciously while maintaining enough analytical distance to document what was happening."

"And instead?"

Julian's expression didn't change. "Instead, the pattern completed. Fully. Permanently. The neural pathways that the sonnet engages became fixed, not temporarily activated but structurally altered. The cycle became self-sustaining."

Lena looked back at Daniel. At his perfect breathing. At his silent, ceaselessly moving lips. At the man who had believed, as she believed, that understanding the mechanism would protect him from it.

"He can hear us?" she asked.

"We believe so. Auditory processing appears intact. He simply does not prioritize external stimuli over the internal pattern."

"Because the pattern gives him something external stimuli don't," Lena said. It wasn't a question.

"Yes."

"What?"

Julian was quiet for a moment. Then: "Completion. The sonnet, in its full form, creates a sensation of resolution so total that everything else becomes noise. Daniel is not in pain. He is not distressed. He is not, in any meaningful sense, suffering. He is simply... finished. The pattern completed itself inside him, and now he has no need for anything that exists outside of it."

Kline's voice was tight. "That's not a person anymore. That's a recording."

"That," Julian said, "is the cost of perfection."

Silence held the room for a long moment. The monitors beeped their steady, indifferent rhythm. Daniel breathed. His lips moved. The cycle continued, as it had continued for three years, as it would continue, Lena understood now, with a clarity that felt like falling, for the rest of his life.

She made herself observe. Made herself catalogue the details with the clinical precision that was her professional obligation and her personal armor. She noted the muscle tone, maintained, not atrophied, which meant the body's autonomic systems were functioning normally even as the conscious mind had retreated into its loop. She noted the skin color, healthy, oxygenated, consistent with adequate circulation. She noted the EEG readout... and stopped.

The brainwave pattern was wrong.

Not wrong as in damaged. Wrong as in *impossible.* The EEG showed sustained, high-amplitude theta waves, the frequency range associated with deep meditation, REM sleep, and the specific neural state that preceded creative insight. But Daniel wasn't meditating. He wasn't sleeping. He was awake, eyes open, in a room with three other people, and his brain was producing the electrical signature of someone in the deepest, most unreachable state of internal focus that neuroscience had a name for.

"His theta activity," Lena said.

"Unprecedented," Julian confirmed. "Dr. Osei, our neuroscientist, has monitored it extensively. The pattern appears to have entrained not just his respiratory and cardiac systems but his neural oscillations themselves. His brain is synchronized to the sonnet's rhythm at the electrical level."

Lena stared at the readout. The implications cascaded through her mind with the relentless momentum of dominoes falling in sequence. If the sonnet could entrain neural oscillations, if it could restructure brainwave patterns through sustained auditory and respiratory synchronization, then it was operating on a level that exceeded anything in the published literature on rhythmic entrainment. This wasn't hypnosis. This wasn't persuasion. This was neurological remodeling.

Kline touched her arm. "We're done here."

She didn't move. Not because she was entranced, her breathing was irregular, her posture deliberately asymmetric, her defenses fully deployed. But because the scientist in her was looking at Daniel Mercer and seeing not just a victim but a *dataset*. A living record of what the sonnet could do when given unlimited access to a human nervous system. Everything she needed to understand the mechanism, really understand it, completely, at the deepest level, was encoded in the body of the man in front of her.

She hated herself for thinking it.

She thought it anyway.

"Lena," Kline said again. Firmer now.

She turned away from the bed. "I'm ready."

They left the room in silence. The door closed behind them with the soft, pneumatic hiss of institutional hardware designed to contain things that shouldn't escape.

In the corridor, Kline stopped walking and turned to face both of them, Lena on one side, Julian on the other, with the squared-off posture of a man who had reached a conclusion and was no longer interested in deliberation.

"We need to shut this down," he said.

Julian regarded him with patient calm. "That is not as simple as it sounds."

"A man is in a permanent coma because of something you did to him. A professor is dead. We've got a murder investigation with no cause of death and a weapon that doesn't leave marks. I don't need it to be simple. I need it to stop."

"Daniel chose his participation," Julian said. "As did Ashcroft. As does every person who attends our events. We are not in the business of coercion, Detective."

"No," Kline said. "You're in the business of making people want things that destroy them. That's worse."

The words landed, and for a moment, just a moment, Julian's composure wavered. Not dramatically. Not visibly, to someone who wasn't watching for it. But Lena, who had spent her career learning to read the involuntary language of the face, saw the microexpression that flickered across his features before his training reasserted control.

Not anger.

Acknowledgment.

As though somewhere beneath the elegant architecture of his justifications, a quieter voice had said the same thing and been overruled.

"I will cooperate with your investigation," Julian said. "Fully. But what I cannot do is unring a bell that has been ringing for three hundred years."

Kline looked at Lena. "Your call."

Lena stood in the corridor between the detective who wanted answers and the man who had them, and she felt the weight of the decision settle onto her the way weather settled onto a landscape, slowly, completely, without asking permission.

"We need more information before we can act," she said. "About the Order, about its members, about the full scope of the sonnet's history and deployment. Shutting it down without understanding it means we're just closing one door while others stay open."

Kline's jaw tightened, but he nodded. He didn't like it. But he trusted her.

Julian inclined his head. "I will make our archives available to you."

"Not just the archives," Lena said. "Everything. Every recording, every research file, every piece of data your Dr. Osei has collected. And I want access to Daniel Mercer's full medical history."

Julian studied her for a moment, and what Lena saw in his eyes was not resistance but something more complex, the expression of a man who had just watched someone take a step deeper into his world and was not entirely sure whether to be pleased or afraid.

"Agreed," he said.

They left the building separately. Kline drove. Lena sat in the passenger seat and watched the city pass and did not speak for eleven blocks.

When she finally broke the silence, her voice was quiet.

"He's going to get worse."

Kline glanced at her. "Who, Daniel?"

"Harris. Harris Cole." She turned to look at him. "He heard fragments in Ashcroft's office. He completed a phrase he never consciously heard. He's already showing signs of anticipation-seeking behavior, the breathing patterns, the compensatory stillness, the cognitive gaps."

Kline's hands tightened on the wheel. "How long?"

"I don't know. Weeks, maybe. Months if he's lucky." She paused. "He's not Daniel, his exposure was minimal, fragmentary. But the mechanism is the same. The craving starts with a gap. An unfinished pattern. And the brain, which cannot tolerate incompleteness, begins reaching for resolution."

"Can you help him?"

Lena looked out the window.

"I don't know yet," she said.

But what she was really thinking, what she couldn't say aloud, not to Kline, not to anyone, was that she understood Harris Cole's craving with a precision that went beyond professional empathy. Because she had felt it too. In the evidence lab, when the first line of the sonnet had adjusted her breathing without permission. During Julian's performance, when the warmth had spread through her chest. In her apartment, humming a rhythm she hadn't chosen.

The sonnet had touched her. Briefly, partially, at the margins. And each time, she'd broken it. Cleanly, professionally, with the trained discipline of a woman who understood the mechanism and refused to be governed by it.

But each time, the breaking had required a little more effort.

And each time, the thing she'd broken had left a slightly deeper impression.

She closed her eyes and leaned her head against the cold glass of the car window, and in the darkness behind her eyelids, unbidden but undeniable, the rhythm was there. Waiting. Patient. Not pushing. Not pulling.

Just present.

The way a current was present in a river, invisible, constant, and perfectly content to wait for you to stop swimming against it.

• • •

CHAPTER EIGHT: *The Cost of Knowing*

Lena locked the door.

Not because she was afraid of interruption, it was past ten on a Thursday night, and the building was empty except for the distant insistence of the heating system and the occasional creak of a structure settling into its own age. She locked the door because what she was about to do required conditions she could control, and a locked door was the simplest form of containment she knew.

Her office looked the same as it always did: bookshelves, desk, lamp, the framed quote about manipulation that Marcus had hated and that she had kept as a kind of philosophical scarecrow, a warning posted at the boundary of her attention. *The most effective manipulation is the kind that feels like your own idea.* She read it now, as she did most nights, and felt its weight settle into a slightly different configuration, not the abstract, academic weight it usually carried, but something more personal, more immediate. More like a mirror than a signpost.

She placed her bag on the desk. Retrieved the notes she'd copied from Ashcroft's archive, not the originals, which remained in evidence, but her own transcriptions, written by hand in a deliberate, unhurried script that bore no resemblance to Ashcroft's increasingly frantic marginalia. Clean copies. Sanitized of the previous writer's urgency. Stripped down to the words themselves.

Fragments.

That was all she had, pieces of something that had been deliberately broken apart and scattered across centuries, like the shards of a mirror that had been smashed not in anger but in caution, by someone who understood that the complete reflection was too dangerous to preserve in one piece.

She arranged them on the desk. Six fragments, each one a cluster of syllables she'd extracted from different sources: the carved line from Ashcroft's desk, the faded marginalia in the reproduction quarto, the partial lines from the hallway audio, the words she'd read from Daniel Mercer's lips. They didn't form a continuous text, there were gaps, silences, places where the poem disappeared into history and hadn't yet been found. But they were enough to suggest a shape. A rhythm. An architecture.

Lena opened the metronome app on her phone.

She set it to 92 beats per minute, deliberately off-sync from the standard resting respiratory rate, which sat between twelve and sixteen cycles per minute. At 92 bpm, the metronome's clicks would interfere with any cadence that tried to align with her breathing, creating a constant, low-level rhythmic disruption that should prevent the entrainment mechanism from engaging.

Should.

She pressed start. The clicks began: sharp, precise, metronomic. A clean, mechanical rhythm with no emotional content, no harmonic richness, no warmth. The rhythmic equivalent of white walls and fluorescent light.

She picked up the first fragment.

When breath becomes command, the body obeys.

She read it silently first. Familiar now. She'd encountered this line four times, in the desk carving, in the audio, in Harris's involuntary completion, and in her own notes. Each encounter had left a slightly deeper impression, like footsteps in softening ground. She knew its rhythm. She knew its weight. She knew the exact point in the sentence where her respiratory system wanted to align and the exact effort required to prevent it.

Then she read it aloud.

Quietly. Not performing, analyzing. The metronome clicked in the background, its mechanical beat a deliberate counterweight to whatever the words might try to do.

"When breath becomes command, the body obeys."

The words felt different spoken.

It was the first thing she noticed, and it was significant enough to make her pause. Reading silently, the line had been an object, a sequence of characters arranged on a page, accessible to analysis, available for dissection. Speaking it gave it a body. Her own body. Her breath shaped the vowels, her tongue placed the consonants, her diaphragm provided the force that turned printed symbols into sound, and in doing so, the line stopped being something she was *examining* and became something she was *performing*.

She reached for the second fragment. This one was from the quarto marginalia, the faded, centuries-old handwriting that she'd read just long enough to feel her lungs adjust before slamming the book shut.

When breath is lent to shape the yielding ear,

And cadence binds what reason would defy—

The metronome clicked. 92 bpm. Steady, indifferent, reliable.

Lena read the lines aloud.

"When breath is lent to shape the yielding ear, and cadence binds what reason would defy—"

The words landed in the room with more weight than their syllable count justified. Each one carried not just meaning but *mass*, a physical presence in the air that she could feel against her face the way you could feel the vibration of a cello string from across a room. The iambic rhythm drove them forward with the quiet insistence of a heartbeat, and her own heart, traitor, always a traitor, reached for the pattern like a hand reaching for a railing in the dark.

The metronome clicked, and Lena held onto it. Anchored her breathing to the mechanical beat. Kept her diaphragm locked to 92 bpm, off-rhythm, unaligned, stubbornly mechanical in the face of something that was asking her to be anything but.

She set the quarto fragment down and picked up the next one.

The lines Daniel Mercer's lips had been forming. The ones she'd read from his face in that quiet, terrible room where a man sat breathing in perfect iambic pentameter while the world went on without him.

So speak me slow, and let resistance part—

She read it aloud.

"So speak me slow, and let resistance part—"

The metronome clicked.

But the metronome was further away now.

Not physically. Perceptually. The mechanical beat hadn't changed, still 92 bpm, still sharp, still precise, but its authority in her attention had diminished. Something else was asking for priority. Something warmer, more resonant, more *interesting* than the flat, emotionless tick of a machine. The words she'd just spoken had created a space in her chest that felt like the space between two notes of a chord that hadn't resolved yet, an openness, a waiting, a gentle, patient expectation that the next sound would complete something that desperately wanted to be completed.

Lena felt the warmth.

It arrived without announcement. A quiet, spreading heat behind her sternum, her body beginning to lower its defenses, not because they'd been breached but because something on the other side of them was offering a very persuasive reason to open the door.

It felt good.

That was the part that shattered something inside her. Not the mechanics, she understood the mechanics. What shattered her was that it felt *good*. Not in the crude, obvious way that drugs felt good or that manipulative flattery felt good, in a deeper, more specific way, the way a perfectly tuned chord felt good, the way being truly understood by another person felt good. The sonnet wasn't offering her pleasure as a bribe. It was offering her precision. The experience of every cell in her body operating in perfect synchronization with an external rhythm that knew exactly what frequency she resonated at.

She wanted to continue.

The realization broke the surface of her consciousness like a fish breaking the surface of a pond: a sudden, startling appearance of something that had been moving underneath for longer than she'd known. She wanted to read the next fragment. She wanted to feel the cadence build. She wanted to follow the pattern to its resolution, to let the architecture of the sonnet complete itself inside her nervous system the way a building completed itself around its foundation, inevitably, beautifully, with the quiet satisfaction of something assuming the shape it was always meant to have.

She wanted to know what the end felt like.

Lena set the page face-down on the desk.

The movement was deliberate, precise, and cost her more than anything she'd done in years. Not physically, the page weighed nothing, her hand moved with its usual competence, the gesture was as simple as turning over a playing card. But cognitively, it was like stopping mid-sentence in a conversation she'd been waiting her whole life to have. The incomplete pattern screamed for resolution. Her nervous system, which had been gently, expertly primed for the next beat in the sequence, found nothing, and the nothing hurt. Not acutely, not dramatically, but with the dull, persistent ache of something unfinished, the way a song stuck in your head hurt when you couldn't remember the last note.

She reached for the metronome.

Turned it off.

Silence fell into the room like a physical weight, and Lena sat inside it and breathed.

Irregular. Deliberate. Ugly. The anti-rhythm of a woman fighting her own biology with the only tools she had left: awareness and refusal.

The warmth faded. Slowly. Reluctantly. Like a guest leaving a party they hadn't wanted to end.

Lena sat in the dark for a long time after that.

Not thinking. Not analyzing. Not doing any of the things she did professionally when confronted with a phenomenon she needed to understand. Just sitting. Breathing. Feeling the absence of the warmth and noting, with the merciless honesty that was both her greatest asset and her deepest wound, that the absence felt worse than the warmth had felt good.

She thought about Marcus, who had used a cruder version of these techniques to manage their marriage for three years, and about how she'd hated him not for the manipulation but for the way he'd made her enjoy it, the way he'd made compliance feel like intimacy, control feel like care, surrender feel like love.

She thought about Julian Calder, watching her resist the thing he spent his life perfecting, and the look in his eyes that she recognized now as the look of a man who had found the one listener he couldn't reach and wanted her more because of it.

And she thought about the warmth, and how easy it would be, how *obscenely* easy, to pick the page back up and keep reading.

She didn't.

She gathered the fragments, placed them in a folder, filed the folder in her desk drawer, and locked the drawer. Then she stood, put on her coat, turned off the lamp, and stood in the darkness of her office with her hand on the door handle and made a rule.

No more solo exposure. No more reading fragments aloud alone, without safeguards, without someone to pull her back. No more treating the sonnet as an object of analysis when her body had made it very clear that it experienced the sonnet as something else entirely.

The rule was rational. It was prudent. It was exactly the kind of boundary a responsible researcher established when they realized they were no longer objective about their subject.

But standing in the dark, hand on the door, Lena Marchetti allowed herself one moment of absolute, undefended honesty.

She had wanted to continue.

Not intellectually. Not professionally. Not because the data demanded it.

She had wanted to continue the way you wanted to lean into a kiss that hadn't happened yet, with the full, aching, undeniable desire of a body that had been offered exactly what it needed and told no.

She opened the door. Walked into the hallway. Locked the office behind her.

And left the fragments in the drawer, where they lay in the dark, patient and precise, waiting, as they had waited for centuries, for someone willing to finish what they'd started.

• • •

CHAPTER NINE: *The Second Body*

The call came on a Monday, which Lena had always considered the most dishonest day of the week, a day that pretended to be a fresh start when it was really just the old week wearing a clean shirt.

Kline rang at six-forty in the morning, which meant someone was dead, because Kline observed a strict professional taxonomy of phone call timing: before seven meant a body, before nine meant a development, after noon meant paperwork.

"Same profile," he said when she picked up. No greeting, no preamble. "Female, late twenties. Found in her apartment in Morningside Heights. No cause, no struggle, no sign of forced entry. Expression on her face—"

"Relief," Lena said.

A pause on the line. "Yeah. How'd you know?"

Lena was already reaching for her coat. "Because whatever happened to Ashcroft didn't stay in his office."

The victim's name was Priya Dasgupta. Twenty-seven years old. Second-year doctoral student in comparative literature at Columbia, with a focus on Renaissance poetry and its relationship to early theories of rhetoric and persuasion. Her apartment was a studio on West 121st Street, small, cluttered with the intellectual debris of a life lived primarily in books, and very, very still.

Lena stood in the doorway and read the room.

The body was in the desk chair, positioned in a way that echoed Ashcroft's scene so precisely that for a disorienting moment, Lena felt as though she'd walked back into the same crime scene wearing different clothes. Priya sat upright, hands resting on the desk, posture relaxed, eyes open, face arranged in the same expression of peaceful, unmistakable release. No defensive wounds. No signs of distress. No evidence that anything had interrupted her work except the quiet, inexplicable cessation of her heartbeat.

The desk was covered in papers, academic, not personal. Printouts of articles, handwritten notes in a tight, efficient script, open books with passages highlighted in multiple colors. A laptop, still open, its screen dark with the power-saving timeout of a machine that hadn't been touched in approximately thirty-six hours, according to the ME's preliminary estimate of time of death.

"No connection to Ashcroft," Kline said, standing beside her with his notebook open. "Different department, different advisor, different research area. We checked, they never co-authored, never shared a committee, never even took the same elevator as far as building access logs show."

"But she studied Renaissance rhetoric," Lena said.

"Yeah. Which puts her in the same intellectual zip code, if not the same address."

Lena moved to the desk. Carefully, with gloved hands, she began examining the papers. Academic articles on persuasion theory. A marked-up copy of George Puttenham's *Arte of English Poesie*. Notes on the physiological effects of meter, which was close enough to Ashcroft's specialty to make her pulse quicken, though not close enough to constitute a direct overlap.

And then she found the laptop.

Kline had the tech team wake the screen. Priya's browser history loaded: the usual mix of academic databases, email, social media, university portals. But in the last forty-eight hours before her death, a new thread had appeared, a sequence of visits to a forum Lena didn't recognize, buried in the deep architecture of a literary discussion site that catered to a niche audience of poetry scholars and enthusiasts.

"Pull up the forum posts," Lena said.

The technician navigated to the thread. It was short, eight posts, each by a different user, none with identifiable profile information. The subject line was innocuous:

On the phonetic structure of unpublished Elizabethan verse

Lena scanned the posts. They appeared, at first, to be a typical academic discussion, references to prosodic analysis, debates about syllabic stress patterns, the kind of granular scholarly argument that would put ninety-nine percent of the population to sleep within two paragraphs.

But the eighth post was different.

It contained no argument. No analysis. No citation. Just four lines of text, formatted with specific spacing, wider gaps between words, deliberate line breaks, a visual rhythm that suggested the text had been arranged not for reading but for *performing*.

Lena didn't read the lines. Not yet. She'd learned that lesson.

Instead, she analyzed the formatting. The spacing between words was irregular in a way that was clearly intentional, some gaps wider, some narrower, creating a visual pattern that implied cadence. If you read the text at the pace the spacing suggested, your voice would naturally fall into a rhythm. And that rhythm, Lena recognized with the cold certainty of someone finding a fingerprint at a crime scene, was the same rhythm she'd heard in the hallway recording, felt in Julian's delivery, fought in her own office.

"Someone posted a fragment of the sonnet," she said.

Kline leaned over her shoulder. "On a public forum?"

"A niche one. Low traffic, specialized audience. But yes, public." She pointed at the spacing. "Look at the formatting. This isn't how you display text for discussion. This is how you display text for effect. The spacing implies cadence. If she read this aloud—"

"She'd be performing it without knowing what she was doing," Kline finished.

Lena nodded. "A fragment. Not enough to induce the full cascade. But enough to create the craving, the anticipation loop. She would have felt restless. Preoccupied. Drawn back to the text again and again, trying to understand why it felt significant."

"And then?"

Lena looked at Priya Dasgupta's body. At the expression of relief. At the stillness that had no clinical explanation.

"And then she found more," she said. "Or more found her."

Kline straightened. His expression had shifted from the procedural focus of a detective processing a scene to something harder, colder, the face of a man who had just realized the scope of his problem was larger than the case file could contain.

"Someone's seeding these fragments," he said.

"Yes."

"Publicly."

"Yes."

"Which means this isn't just the Order. This is someone spreading it."

Lena looked at the forum post on the screen. At the careful formatting, the deliberate spacing, the weaponized typography that turned an internet text post into a neurological tripwire.

"Not spreading it," she said. "Distributing it. There's a difference. This is controlled. Targeted. Someone who understands the mechanism is placing fragments in spaces where the right kind of person, someone who studies language, who reads aloud as part of their work, who is predisposed to engage deeply with poetic structure, will encounter them."

"Why? To recruit?"

"To create need." Lena straightened. "Think about it. If you want people to seek out the Cadence Society, you don't advertise. You create a craving they can't satisfy on their own. You give them just enough to feel something they've never felt before, and then you let their own neurology do the rest. They'll come looking. They always come looking."

Kline's jaw tightened. "And the ones who find too much before they find the Order?"

Lena looked at Priya.

"They end up here," she said.

She spent the rest of the morning reconstructing Priya's last days. The browser history told a story that was, in its own way, more disturbing than the body. After encountering the forum post, Priya had searched for related content, other fragments, other discussions, other threads where similar text might appear. She'd found two more, different forums, different platforms, same formatting. Same deliberate spacing. Same implied cadence.

Over the next thirty-six hours, she'd visited these pages a combined nineteen times. The visits grew more frequent as the hours passed, the gaps between them shortening from hours to minutes, the pattern of obsessive return that Lena recognized from the clinical literature on compulsive behavior, but mapped, in this case, not onto a substance or a gambling algorithm but onto the specific, maddening, irresistible incompleteness of a pattern that wanted to be finished.

At some point, the browser history couldn't tell her exactly when, Priya had read the fragments aloud. Perhaps she'd done it as part of her academic process, sounding out the prosody to analyze its structure. Perhaps she'd done it because the restlessness had become unbearable and her body was telling her, in the only language bodies knew, that the relief she needed was in the rhythm of those words.

Either way, she'd performed the fragments. In her apartment. Alone. Without understanding what she was doing.

And the fragments had done what fragments always did.

They'd reached for completion.

Lena left the apartment with a copy of the forum posts sealed in an evidence bag and a feeling in her chest that was not warmth, not the seductive, pleasurable warmth of the sonnet's effect, but something colder and more urgent. The feeling of watching a fire spread from one building to the next and realizing that the fire department didn't know what it was fighting.

In the car, she told Kline what she needed.

"I need to talk to Julian again. This distribution, he has to know about it. Either it's coming from inside the Order, or someone outside has gotten their hands on fragments and is deploying them independently."

Kline drummed his fingers on the steering wheel. "You trust him to tell you the truth?"

Lena considered the question with the seriousness it deserved.

"I trust him to tell me something useful," she said. "Truth is a different category."

Kline nodded. "Fair enough." He pulled into traffic. "But for the record, a second body changes the math. This isn't academic anymore. Someone is dying because of this thing, and the people who understand it best are the people who've been playing with it the longest."

Lena didn't argue. He was right. The investigation had shifted from a single unexplained death to a pattern of casualties that shared no connection except the invisible thread of a rhythm designed to bypass every defense the human mind had evolved.

She looked out the window at the city, at the millions of people going about their Monday, reading words on screens, listening to voices in earbuds, absorbing language in quantities that no previous generation of humans had ever processed, and she thought about how easy it would be for a few carefully formatted lines of text to slip into that river of information and float downstream into the neurology of someone who didn't know they were vulnerable.

And for the first time since the investigation began, Lena Marchetti was not just concerned.

She was afraid.

• • •

CHAPTER TEN: *The Salon*

The estate sat on twelve acres in northern Westchester, behind a gate that opened without being asked and a driveway that curved through bare November oaks with the deliberate grace of a sentence that knew exactly where it was going.

Julian had arranged the invitation. Two days after Priya Dasgupta's death, Lena had demanded answers about the online fragments, and Julian had offered something better: access. A Cadence Society gathering. A salon, as the members called it, the polite, cultivated word for what Lena suspected was closer to a ritual, or a drug deal, or the most sophisticated form of recreational surrender she'd ever encountered.

"You will attend as a new Listener," Julian had said. "Observe everything. Participate in nothing. If at any point you feel the effect engaging, leave immediately."

"And if I can't?"

He'd paused, the kind of pause that, from anyone else, would have been dramatic but from Julian felt like genuine consideration. "Then I will remove you myself."

Kline had argued against it. Loudly, articulately, and with the creative profanity of a man who'd spent twenty years in precincts where diplomacy was optional. In the end, he'd agreed to park a block away with his phone on and a very clear understanding of the address, the layout, and the number of minutes he would wait before entering the building uninvited with his badge and his extremely visible displeasure.

Lena arrived alone.

The house was beautiful in the way that very old money was beautiful, not showy, not modern, not trying to impress anyone who hadn't already been impressed by the family name attached to the property tax records. Stone walls. Tall windows. Interior lighting that suggested candlelight without committing to it. A foyer paneled in dark wood where a young woman in a simple black dress took Lena's coat with a smile that was warm, genuine, and utterly unsurprised by her arrival.

"Through the hall," the woman said. "The garden room."

Lena followed the hallway toward a pair of glass doors that opened onto a space she hadn't expected. Not a drawing room or a parlor or any of the formal settings she'd imagined for a secret society's gathering. A conservatory, glass-walled, high-ceilinged, filled with the architectural green of carefully maintained plants and the amber glow of low, strategically placed lighting. The acoustics were immediately apparent: the glass walls would reflect sound, the plants would absorb excess reverberation, and the high ceiling would allow low-frequency resonance to develop fully before reaching the listener's ear. It was a room designed for the human voice the way a concert hall was designed for an orchestra, every surface, every angle, every material chosen for its contribution to the sound.

There were approximately thirty people inside.

Lena's first impression was of ease. Not the forced ease of a cocktail party or the performative ease of a corporate retreat, but a genuine, physical ease that was visible in the posture of every person in the room. Shoulders were down. Jaws were loose. Breathing was slow and regular. People stood in small groups, conversing quietly, holding wine glasses with the relaxed grip of hands that had forgotten about vigilance. They were beautiful, not uniformly, not artificially, but in the specific way that relaxed, well-nourished, genuinely content people were beautiful. The beauty of lowered defenses.

She recognized the signatures of prior exposure immediately. These were not newcomers. These were Listeners, regular attendees who had been conditioned, over multiple sessions, to associate this environment with the specific neurological state the sonnet induced. They didn't need to hear the words to begin responding. The room itself was a trigger. The lighting, the acoustics, the company of other people who shared the same association, all of it combined to create a priming effect that was already lowering their resistance before the performance had begun.

Lena moved through the room with the studied casualness of someone who belonged, accepting a glass of wine she had no intention of drinking and positioning herself near the back wall where she could observe without being observed. She maintained her asymmetric posture. She kept her breathing irregular. She made herself into a stone in the middle of a river, letting the current of the room's collective rhythm flow around her without carrying her with it.

A man beside her, mid-fifties, silver-haired, impeccably dressed, leaned slightly toward her. Not aggressively. Not invasively. With the gentle, conspiratorial intimacy of someone sharing a secret at a party.

"First time?" he asked.

"That obvious?"

He smiled. "You're standing like someone waiting for a train. Everyone else is standing like the train has already arrived." He extended his hand. "Thomas."

"Elena," Lena lied, using the name Julian had provided for her cover.

Thomas studied her with an intelligence that was sharper than his casual posture suggested. "You'll enjoy tonight. Margaux is performing."

The name registered. Julian had mentioned a Margaux, one of the Order's trained practitioners, a vocalist who could deliver fragments of the sonnet with enough precision to produce measurable effects.

"I've heard good things," Lena said, because that seemed like something a new Listener would say.

Thomas's smile deepened. "Good things. Yes. That's one way to describe it." He took a sip of his wine and looked across the room with the anticipatory pleasure of a man settling into a theater seat. "The first time is always the most intense. After that, you'll come back because you remember what it felt like. But the first time, that's the one you'll carry."

Lena filed his words, noted his breathing rate, twelve cycles per minute, slightly below normal rest, consistent with conditioned parasympathetic priming, and returned her attention to the room.

At the far end of the conservatory, a space had been cleared. No stage. No podium. No separation between performer and audience beyond a few feet of empty floor and the acoustic architecture of the room itself. A single chair stood in the cleared space, angled to face the gathered Listeners, and beside it, standing, not seated, with the poised stillness of a woman who understood that performance began before the first word, was Margaux Levine.

She was striking. Not in the polished, geometrical way of magazine covers, but in the way that a cello was striking, all curves and warmth and the suggestion of sound waiting to be released. Dark hair, loose around her shoulders. Eyes that moved across the room with the focused attention of someone who saw not individuals but an audience, a collective nervous system that she was about to address with the oldest instrument humans possessed.

The room settled. Not because anyone signaled for silence, but because something in the collective attention shifted, a gravitational pull toward the cleared space, a consensual turning of focus that happened the way weather happened: gradually, inevitably, without anyone deciding it should.

Margaux did not speak immediately.

She breathed.

Lena watched her ribcage expand, slowly, fully, with the controlled, preparatory intake of a trained vocalist filling her lungs not with air but with intention. The exhale was equally measured, equally deliberate, and Lena felt the room respond to it: thirty bodies unconsciously adjusting their own breathing to match, the way a room full of sleeping infants would synchronize their breathing to the mother's respiratory rhythm. The priming was already deep enough that Margaux's breath alone was an instrument.

Then she spoke.

Not the sonnet. Not directly. Something adjacent, a passage that shared the sonnet's metric structure and phonetic profile without being the sonnet itself. A preparatory text, a warm-up act, a door opened partway to let the listener's neurology peek through before being asked to walk through.

Lena didn't process the words. She processed the effect.

Around her, the room softened. She could see it happening in real time, the progressive surrender of thirty nervous systems to a single vocal rhythm, the collective lowering of defenses that looked, from the outside, like a room full of people falling in love at the same time. Postures opened. Faces relaxed. Breathing deepened and synchronized until the room was no longer a collection of individual respiratory systems but a single organism, rising and falling together, powered by the cadence of one woman's voice.

The man beside her, Thomas, closed his eyes. His wine glass hung from fingers that had forgotten they were holding anything. His breathing had dropped to ten cycles per minute, and the expression on his face was the expression of someone experiencing a pleasure so specific and so total that describing it would require inventing a new vocabulary.

Lena maintained her position. Asymmetric. Irregular. Controlled.

But the room was pressing at her now. Not physically, acoustically. Thirty synchronized nervous systems produced a collective rhythm that was far more powerful than any individual delivery. It was the difference between a single voice and a choir: not louder, but *deeper*, the fundamental frequency reinforced by harmonics that thickened the air and made resistance feel less like discipline and more like stubbornness.

Her breathing shifted. She caught it, corrected it, but the correction was harder than it had been in Julian's room, harder than it had been in her office, harder than it had been at any point in the investigation. The collective entrainment of the room was a force multiplier, and it pressed against her defenses with the gentle, relentless persistence of water finding its way through cracks in stone.

Margaux's voice moved deeper into the preparatory text. The cadence tightened. The pauses shortened. The anticipation built, not in Lena's mind, which remained analytical and vigilant, but in her *body*, which was responding to the acoustic environment with the automatic, autonomic honesty of an instrument being played by thirty invisible hands.

Warmth. In her chest. Behind her sternum. Not the subtle, tentative warmth of the evidence lab or her office. A fuller warmth, a deeper warmth, the warmth of a body surrounded by other bodies all moving in the same direction, all breathing the same rhythm, all surrendering to the same invitation. It was the warmth of belonging. The warmth of being part of something larger than yourself. The warmth of letting go.

Thomas leaned toward her without opening his eyes. His voice was a murmur, barely audible above Margaux's delivery, but the words landed with the precision of something that had been waiting to be said.

"It's easier," he whispered, "if you don't fight."

Lena's hands tightened at her sides.

She looked at the room. At the thirty people breathing in unison. At their open faces, their lowered defenses, their willing, grateful, terrifying surrender. At Margaux, whose voice moved through them like light through glass, not blocked, not resisted, simply *admitted*, the way a window admitted the sun.

And she felt, with a clarity that cut through every layer of her professional armor, the exact shape of the choice in front of her.

She could stay. Let the collective rhythm carry her. Let the warmth expand. Let her breathing synchronize with thirty other nervous systems and experience what Thomas and the others experienced, the thing they came back for, the thing that made them beautiful, the thing that filled their faces with that specific, devastating ease.

Or she could leave.

She left.

Through the conservatory doors. Down the hallway. Past the woman with the coat. Out the front door and into the cold November dark where the air was irregular and uncontrolled and full of the natural, unmanaged chaos of wind and traffic and the particular acoustic disorder of the world outside.

She walked to the end of the driveway. Her breathing was ragged. Not from exertion. From effort, the sustained, exhausting, increasingly costly effort of refusing something that every cell in her body wanted to accept.

Kline's car was parked on the street. She got in, closed the door, and sat in the passenger seat breathing hard while Kline watched her without speaking.

After a full minute, he said: "Bad?"

"Bad," she confirmed.

"How bad?"

Lena closed her eyes. In the darkness behind her eyelids, the warmth was still there, fading, but present, like the afterimage of a bright light. And beneath it, fainter but more persistent, the rhythm. Always the rhythm.

"I need to move faster," she said. "Before the next person reads the wrong thing in the wrong place and doesn't wake up."

Kline started the engine without another word.

But Thomas's whisper followed her home. Through the car ride, through the locked door, through the shower and thc coffee and the three a.m. silence of her apartment.

It's easier if you don't fight.

She knew he was wrong.

She was beginning to understand that he might also be right.

• • •

CHAPTER ELEVEN: *The Corrupted Version*

The package was waiting in her department mailbox when Lena arrived at Columbia the next morning, which meant someone knew her academic schedule well enough to time a delivery for maximum impact. A manila envelope, unmarked, unsealed, containing a single sheet of paper and a handwritten note in an unfamiliar hand:

This version is circulating. It is not ours. Be careful.

No signature. But the paper stock was the same heavy cream as Julian's original invitation, which told her everything she needed to know about the sender while telling her nothing she could prove.

Lena took the envelope to her office, locked the door, and examined the sheet of paper without reading the text.

The formatting was immediately familiar, the same deliberate spacing, the same implied cadence that she'd found on the forum post in Priya Dasgupta's browser history. But the arrangement was different. Where the sonnet fragments she'd encountered before had been structured for a warm, building rhythm, the parasympathetic cascade of calm and compliance, this version's spacing suggested something else entirely.

The gaps between words were shorter. Tighter. The line breaks came at unexpected intervals, creating a visual rhythm that felt not like breathing but like breathing interrupted, a stuttering, accelerating pattern that would produce not relaxation but activation. Not warmth but heat. Not ease but urgency.

Lena recognized the principle. It was the same mechanism, rhythmic entrainment through visual cadence, but tuned to a different frequency. If the original sonnet targeted the parasympathetic nervous system, this version targeted the sympathetic. Fight or flight. Adrenaline. Cortisol. The neurochemistry of threat.

She read the four lines through a sheet of translucent drafting paper, which blurred the text enough to prevent her from engaging with the cadence while allowing her to identify the words.

When breath is wrung from those who cannot speak,

And silence screams what terror will not say,

The pulse remembers every wound, each break,

And learns at last the sharpness of obey.

She recognized fragments of the original. *When breath*, the opening construction. *The pulse*, from the third line. *Learns at last*, the fourth. But the words between them had been changed, and the changes were not random. Someone had taken the sonnet's architecture, its metric structure, its phonetic profile, its specific arrangement of stressed and unstressed syllables, and refilled it with different content the way you might pour different liquid into the same glass.

The glass was the same. The liquid was poison.

Lena set the paper down and sat with the implications for a long time.

The sonnet could be *tuned.*

This was not in Ashcroft's notes. It was not in Julian's explanation. It was not in any of the material she'd reviewed from the Order's archives, which Julian had begun sharing with her in carefully curated installments, enough to be useful, not enough to be comprehensive. Either the Order didn't know this was possible, or they knew and hadn't told her.

Either way, the implications were staggering.

If the mechanism was the cadence rather than the content, if the rhythmic structure was the weapon and the words were merely the delivery vehicle, then the sonnet was not a single artifact. It was a *template.* A framework that could be filled with any content, tuned to any emotional frequency, aimed at any neurological target. You could write a version that induced calm, or fear, or rage, or grief, or desire, or loyalty. You could, if you understood the architecture well enough, create a version for every emotional state the human nervous system was capable of producing.

Lena picked up her phone and called Julian.

He answered on the second ring, which was unusual, he typically let calls ring four or five times, maintaining control over even the micro-dynamics of a phone conversation. The rapid pickup suggested he'd been expecting her call.

"You've seen it," he said.

"I've seen it. Who made it?"

A pause. Longer than his standard calibrated pauses. This one carried actual uncertainty, which from Julian was the equivalent of another person shouting.

"We don't know," he said. "It appeared approximately two months ago, circulating in literary forums and poetry communities. The formatting is precise enough that whoever created it understands the underlying mechanism. But the emotional target is antithetical to everything the Order has ever developed."

"It induces fear," Lena said.

"Yes. And more than fear. Our researcher, Dr. Osei, obtained a copy and had two volunteer subjects read it aloud under controlled conditions. Both reported acute anxiety, elevated heart rate, a persistent sense of being watched or followed. One subject experienced a panic attack that lasted forty minutes."

"From reading four lines of poetry."

"From reading four lines of poetry in a rhythm designed to hijack the sympathetic nervous system. Yes."

Lena looked at the sheet on her desk. At the words that sat in their careful, terrible formatting like a loaded weapon displayed in a museum case.

"Julian. If the mechanism can be tuned to different emotional frequencies, then the original sonnet isn't unique. It's a proof of concept."

Silence on the line. The kind of silence that happened when someone heard a truth they'd been avoiding spoken aloud for the first time.

"Yes," Julian said finally.

"And anyone who understands the rhythmic architecture can create variants."

"In theory."

"Not in theory. In practice. Someone already has."

Another pause. Then, carefully: "This is why I sent it to you. Because you are the only person outside the Order with the expertise to analyze the variant and the discipline to do so safely."

"And because you need my help."

Julian was quiet for a moment. When he spoke again, the careful calibration of his voice had slipped, just fractionally, just enough for Lena to hear something beneath the performance that sounded, for the first time, like honesty.

"Yes," he said. "I need your help."

Lena sat with that for a moment. Julian Calder, the most controlled person she had ever met, a man who deployed silence the way other people deployed artillery, had just admitted need. The admission was itself a kind of vulnerability, and vulnerability from Julian was as disorienting as calm from a hurricane.

"I have conditions," she said.

"Name them."

"Full access to Dr. Osei and her data. Not curated installments, everything. Brain scans, physiological recordings, listener classification studies, every piece of research the Order has ever produced."

"Agreed."

"And I want to see your archives. The historical material. The original fragments, the marginalia, the correspondence, everything that traces the sonnet's history back to its origins."

A longer pause.

"That is a significant request."

"A second person is dead, Julian. Someone is distributing fragments that kill people, and now someone else is building variants that weaponize the mechanism for fear instead of compliance. Your archives aren't sacred anymore. They're evidence."

The line was quiet for five seconds. Lena counted.

"Come tomorrow evening," Julian said. "I'll have everything prepared."

He hung up without saying goodbye, which Lena recognized as a sign that the conversation had cost him more than he wanted her to know.

She put the phone down and looked at the corrupted sonnet one more time.

Fear. Desire. Rage. Compliance. The sonnet wasn't a poem. It was a *grammar*, a set of rules for constructing experiences inside the human nervous system using nothing but the rhythm of the human voice. And like any grammar, once you understood it, you could use it to say anything.

Anything at all.

She locked the variant in her desk drawer, beside the original fragments, and sat in her office while the morning light moved across the wall and the city outside went about its business in blissful, terrible ignorance of the fact that the most dangerous weapon in human history didn't require plutonium or computers or satellite networks.

It required only a voice.

And someone willing to listen.

• • •

CHAPTER TWELVE: *The Conversation*

Julian's private quarters were nothing like his performance space.

Lena had expected more of the same, acoustic engineering, controlled lighting, the deliberate architecture of a room designed to optimize the transmission of the human voice. What she found instead was warmth. Real warmth, not the manufactured kind. A room that looked lived in, books stacked on surfaces rather than shelved, a piano in the corner with sheet music open on the stand, a leather armchair by the window that had been sat in so many thousands of times that it had developed the topography of the body it served. Soft light from table lamps. The smell of coffee and something darker, richer, a trace of cologne or cedar or the particular scent of a man who spent his life surrounded by wood-paneled rooms and old paper.

It was disarming. And Lena recognized, with the cool precision of a woman who had spent her career identifying the mechanics of influence, that the disarming was intentional.

"You're analyzing the room," Julian said from the doorway behind her. He'd stepped out to speak with someone in the corridor, Nadia Osei, Lena suspected, about the archive access she'd demanded, and had returned to find her standing in the center of his living space with the focused attention of an appraiser at an auction.

"Professional habit," she said.

"And your conclusion?"

"You've made this room warm on purpose. Everything in your professional spaces is designed for control, acoustic precision, visual minimalism, environmental management. This room is designed for something else."

"Which is?"

"Trust."

Julian entered the room and closed the door behind him. The sound was soft, not the pneumatic hiss of the performance space's engineered seals but the simple, unremarkable click of a door closing in an old building. Human. Imperfect.

"Trust," he repeated, as though tasting the word. "An interesting accusation."

"Is it inaccurate?"

"It is incomplete." He crossed to a sideboard and poured two glasses of something amber without asking whether she wanted one. "I designed this room for conversation. Real conversation, not the transactional kind that happens in professional settings. Trust is a prerequisite for that, yes. But trust isn't the goal. It's the medium."

He extended a glass to her. She took it, not because she intended to drink, but because refusing would have been a power move, and power moves were the vocabulary of people who didn't trust their other options.

Julian settled into the leather chair with the unselfconscious ease of a man returning to a space that had long since memorized his body. He didn't gesture for her to sit. He waited.

Lena sat in the chair opposite him, approximately five feet away. Close enough for conversation at a natural volume. Far enough for professional distance. The exact interval that would later, she knew, begin to feel like neither.

"You asked for the archives," Julian said. "They'll be available tomorrow. Dr. Osei will walk you through the research database personally."

"Thank you."

"That's not why you're here tonight."

He said it without challenge, without accusation. An observation. The kind of flat, accurate statement that only someone who had been watching you very carefully for a sustained period could make.

Lena held his gaze. "No. It's not."

"Then why?"

She'd been asking herself the same question on the drive over, and the answer she'd arrived at was honest enough to be uncomfortable. "Because you know things about this sonnet that I can't get from archives or data. Things that live in the delivery, in the practice, in the experience of working with it for, how many years?"

"Twenty-three."

"Twenty-three years. More than half your life. That knowledge isn't in your files, Julian. It's in you. And I need it."

Something shifted in his expression, not dramatically, not visibly to anyone who wasn't watching with Lena's specific attention, but present. A softening at the corners of his eyes. A reduction in the subtle tension he carried in his jawline, so habitual and so controlled that most people probably didn't know it existed.

Interest. Not professional interest. Not the calculated interest of a man managing a situation. The genuine, unguarded interest of a human being who had just heard someone describe them with unexpected accuracy.

"What would you like to know?" he asked.

"Why you."

He blinked. "I'm sorry?"

"You were a pianist. A prodigy, from what I've been able to find. Concert career by sixteen, critical acclaim, the kind of trajectory that most musicians would kill for. And you walked away from it to study neurolinguistics and eventually to devote your life to a poem that may or may not have been written by Shakespeare. Why?"

Julian was quiet for a moment. Not his standard calibrated pause, something less controlled, less precise. The silence of a man considering whether to answer a question honestly or strategically, and discovering that the two options were further apart than he'd expected.

"Do you know what it's like," he said, "to sit at a piano and watch an audience cry?"

Lena didn't answer. The question wasn't rhetorical, but it wasn't asking for a response. It was asking for space.

"I was sixteen the first time it happened," he continued. "A recital in Cambridge. Chopin's Ballade No. 1 in G minor. I played it the way I always played, technically precise, dynamically controlled, every phrase shaped according to the score and my teacher's interpretation. And a woman in the third row began to cry. Not theatrically. Quietly. Tears running down her face, her hands loose in her lap, her breathing synchronized with the phrasing of the music as though her body had forgotten how to breathe on its own and was borrowing the rhythm from the piano."

He looked at his hands. They were still, the hands of a man who had once made a room full of strangers weep and had never entirely recovered from the experience.

"I finished the piece. I took my bow. I went backstage. And I spent the next three hours trying to understand what had happened, not to her, but to the *space between us*. How sound waves produced by strings struck by hammers activated by keys depressed by fingers controlled by a brain interpreting marks on a page could cross fifteen feet of air and rearrange the neurology of a stranger."

"And you couldn't," Lena said.

"Not with music. Music was too complex, too variable, too dependent on subjective association and personal history. One listener's Chopin was another listener's background noise. The effect was real but unreliable. Powerful but imprecise."

He looked up at her.

"I wanted precision."

"And you found it."

"The Instrument offered something music never could," he said. "Consistency. Reproducibility. A mechanism that worked not through subjective emotional association but through the fundamental architecture of the human nervous system. Not *this* person's breathing or *that* person's heart rate, the breathing, the heart rate. Universal. Reliable. As precise as physics."

Lena set her untouched glass on the table beside her. "You're describing a weapon."

"I'm describing an instrument. The distinction is in the hand that holds it."

"And your hand has never slipped?"

The question landed, and for a moment the room felt very still. Not the engineered stillness of Julian's performance space, the natural, slightly uncomfortable stillness of a conversation that had arrived at a place neither participant had planned to go.

"Once," Julian said.

Lena waited.

"A woman. Ten years ago. A Listener who had attended several salons and expressed interest in a private session. I agreed. The session was..." He paused, and Lena watched him search for the right word with the care of a man who understood that precision mattered, especially when it was painful. "...excessive. I allowed the cadence to build beyond the parameters I normally maintained. I was curious about the upper limits of the effect, and she was willing, and I told myself that her willingness was sufficient ethical ground."

"What happened?"

"She experienced a compliance state more profound than anything I'd induced before. Complete parasympathetic dominance. Heart rate dropped to forty-two beats per minute. She stopped responding to external stimuli for almost eleven minutes."

"And after?"

Julian's gaze didn't waver, but something behind it did, a tremor in the foundation, the kind of movement that only someone who knew the architecture of his composure would detect.

"She came back," he said. "Physically, she recovered fully. But she was... changed. Not damaged, not in any way she could articulate or I could measure. Just different. As though the boundary I'd pushed past hadn't fully restored itself. She continued attending salons for another year, but the effect of normal sessions was diminished for her. She needed more. The standard cadence wasn't enough anymore. She'd been given a glimpse of something deeper, and everything else felt shallow by comparison."

"An addict," Lena said.

"A connoisseur," Julian corrected, and the word carried an edge of self-disgust that Lena had never heard from him before. "That is the word I used at the time. A connoisseur who had developed a refined palate and could no longer be satisfied by ordinary fare. It sounds elegant, doesn't it? It sounds like a compliment. It took me two years to recognize it for what it actually was."

"Which was?"

"A rationalization for having broken something I didn't know how to fix."

Silence settled between them. Not Julian's deliberate, weaponized silence, something rawer, more uncertain. The silence of a room where two people had stopped performing for each other and were sitting, briefly, in the unmanaged space between their respective masks.

Lena felt something shift inside her that had nothing to do with the sonnet.

It was the particular, dangerous warmth that came from witnessing a powerful person's vulnerability, the intimacy of seeing behind the curtain, of being trusted with the mechanism that drove the machine. She recognized it because she'd felt it before. With Marcus, who had shown her his doubts and his fears and his unfinished thoughts, and who had used that apparent vulnerability as another form of control, the intimacy itself as a chain, the confession as a leash.

But this felt different.

Or she wanted it to feel different, which was not the same thing, and the inability to distinguish between the two was exactly the kind of ambiguity that had gotten her into trouble before.

"My turn," Julian said, and the shift in his voice was subtle but unmistakable, from confessional to curious, from past to present, from his history to hers. "You study manipulation. You've built a career on identifying the mechanisms by which one person controls another through speech. That's not the kind of specialty a person chooses because it sounds interesting at a cocktail party.

That's the kind of specialty a person chooses because they've been on the receiving end."

Lena's fingers tightened slightly around the arm of her chair. "Is this analysis or interrogation?"

"Conversation," Julian said. "Which, between people like us, sometimes resembles both."

She held his gaze and considered her options. She could deflect, she was good at it, better than most, and Julian would accept the deflection with the grace of a man who understood that some doors required more than one attempt. Or she could answer. Honestly. And in doing so, surrender a piece of the advantage she'd been maintaining since they'd first met, the advantage of opacity, of being the one asking questions rather than answering them.

"My ex-husband," she said.

She'd said it before. To Kline, in passing. To her therapist, in clinical detail. To the mirror, in anger. But saying it to Julian, in his warm, disarming, deliberately trustworthy room, felt different. Felt like stepping off a ledge, not because the drop was dangerous but because she didn't know what the ground looked like.

"Marcus was a defense attorney. Brilliant. Charming. The kind of man who walked into a room and rearranged the power dynamics by the time he'd finished saying hello." She paused, and the pause was not calibrated or strategic. It was the pause of a woman deciding how much truth she could afford to part with. "He used speech patterns, cadence modulation, embedded commands, strategic pausing, to manage our marriage for three years. Not aggressively. Not obviously. Lovingly. He did it the way a gardener trains a vine, gently, patiently, shaping the growth without the plant ever realizing it's being shaped."

"And you didn't notice."

"I am the foremost expert in the country on verbal manipulation techniques," Lena said. "And I didn't notice for three years."

She let that sentence sit in the room, let it fill the space between them with its particular weight, and watched Julian receive it. His expression didn't change, not externally. But she saw the way his breathing shifted, the way his body adjusted to accommodate information that had reorganized his understanding of the woman sitting across from him. Not pity. Not sympathy. Something more precise.

Recognition.

"That," he said quietly, "is why you resist."

"Yes."

"Not because you're strong."

"No."

"Because you're afraid."

The word landed like a hand on bare skin, not violent, not aggressive, but *present* in a way that couldn't be ignored. Lena felt it. Felt the accuracy of it. Felt the specific, unbearable vulnerability of being correctly identified by someone who was capable of using the identification as a weapon.

"Yes," she said. "I'm afraid."

The room held still. Not the engineered stillness of acoustic control but the natural, fragile stillness of two people who had arrived, through conversation, at a place that neither of them had furniture for.

Julian leaned forward. Not much. An inch, perhaps two. But the reduction in distance changed the equation in ways that had nothing to do with acoustics and everything to do with the particular physics of two bodies that had become aware of each other as *bodies*, not as minds, not as adversaries, not as professional abstractions, but as warm, breathing, vulnerable, present bodies separated by five feet of air that was beginning to feel like three.

"Lena," he said, and her name in his voice was its own kind of sonnet, two syllables placed with the precision and care of a man who understood that the way you said a name could be the most intimate thing you ever did with your mouth. "You're afraid that if you let go, you'll lose yourself. The way you lost yourself with Marcus. The way you almost lost yourself in my performance room, and at the salon, and in your office alone with the fragments."

She didn't deny it. Couldn't.

"But here is what I think you haven't considered," he continued. "Marcus controlled you without your knowledge. The sonnet influences you against your will. But I am sitting here, in a room with no acoustic engineering and no prepared cadence, speaking to you in my natural voice, at my natural rhythm, and I am asking nothing of your body."

He held her gaze.

"I am asking something of your mind."

The warmth that moved through Lena's chest was not the warmth of the sonnet. It was older than that, deeper than that, more dangerous than that. It was the warmth that preceded desire, not the manufactured desire of neurological manipulation but the organic, unmanaged, deeply human desire that arose when two people recognized each other across the distance of their respective solitudes.

She wanted to lean forward. She wanted to close the distance. She wanted to hear what his voice sounded like when it stopped being precise and became *urgent*, when the control slipped and the man underneath was speaking not to influence but to *reach*.

She didn't.

"What are you asking?" she said, and her voice was steady, which was perhaps the most impressive act of resistance she'd performed since this investigation began.

Julian studied her. His eyes moved across her face with the attention he gave to everything, the granular, intimate attention of a man who experienced the world in higher resolution than most people were capable of. But there was something else in his gaze now. Something she'd never seen before.

Uncertainty.

Not about the sonnet. Not about the investigation. About *her*. About what he wanted from her, and whether wanting it was something his philosophy of control could accommodate.

"I'm asking you," he said, "to consider the possibility that not every form of influence is an assault. That some forms of power are offered, not imposed. That surrender, chosen freely and with full knowledge, is not weakness but the deepest expression of trust a human being is capable of."

Lena's heart rate was elevated. She could feel it, not the steady, measured rhythm of her professional composure but the slightly quickened beat of a body responding to something it hadn't been asked to defend against.

"That's a beautiful argument," she said. "It's also exactly the argument that every person who has ever manipulated another person uses to justify what they've done."

Julian smiled. And for the first time, the smile was not controlled, not placed, not calibrated. It was the sudden, unguarded smile of a man who had been surprised, and who found the surprise more pleasurable than anything he'd planned.

"Yes," he said. "It is."

A beat. Two. The room held its breath.

"And the difference between the version I mean and the version they meant," he added, "is the question I've spent my entire life trying to answer."

Lena stood.

Not abruptly. Not in flight. With the measured deliberation of a woman who knew that if she stayed in that chair for one more minute, she would do something that could not be analyzed or categorized or filed away under *evidence*. Something that existed in the space between the professional and the personal, the clinical and the carnal, the studied and the *felt*.

"Thank you for the evening," she said.

Julian remained seated. He looked up at her with an expression that she could have spent a decade analyzing and never fully decoded, composed and vulnerable, controlled and cracking, the face of a man watching something beautiful leave a room and understanding, for the first time, that he did not have the power to make it stay.

"Lena," he said.

She stopped at the door.

"The archives will be ready in the morning. Dr. Osei will meet you at nine."

She nodded. Opened the door. Stepped into the corridor.

And paused.

Not because she wanted to go back. Because she wanted to remember exactly what it felt like to stand on this side of the threshold, the side where she was still in control, still defended, still the woman who studied influence rather than the woman who succumbed to it.

Because she suspected that the next time she stood in this hallway, she would not be the same person.

She walked to the elevator, pressed the button, and waited.

Behind her, through the door she hadn't fully closed, she heard Julian Calder do something she'd never heard him do before.

He sighed.

Not the controlled, measured exhalation of a man managing his respiratory system.

A sigh. Human. Involuntary. The sound of a man who had just realized that the one instrument he'd spent his life perfecting was completely, utterly useless against the woman who had just walked out of his room.

Lena stepped into the elevator and pressed the lobby button and did not look back.

But she smiled.

Because for the first time in this investigation, Julian Calder had been the one whose breathing was out of rhythm.

• • •

CHAPTER THIRTEEN: *The Fracture*

Lena heard the argument before she saw it.

She'd arrived at Julian's building for her first session with the Order's archives, nine o'clock, as arranged, Dr. Osei waiting in the corridor with a cardboard box of hard drives and the slightly haunted expression of a woman who had been awake for most of the night making copies of things she wasn't sure she should be copying. But the archive session hadn't started, because the corridor was occupied by something more immediate: voices from behind a closed door, one measured and one not, engaged in the kind of confrontation that vibrated through wood and plaster like a tuning fork pressed against bone.

Nadia Osei stood beside her, both of them frozen in the particular awkwardness of people who had been caught eavesdropping by the simple fact of arriving at the wrong time.

"Should we come back?" Lena asked.

Nadia shook her head. "This has been building for weeks. You should hear it." She paused. "You need to hear it."

Through the door, the unmeasured voice, deep, confident, accustomed to boardrooms, cut through the muffled acoustics with the blunt efficiency of a man who had spent his life buying things and was frustrated to encounter something that wasn't for sale.

"—three hundred years of refinement, Julian, and you want to keep it in a parlor trick? Private salons for thirty people? That's not preservation. That's a hobby."

Victor Hale. Lena had been briefed on him by Kline, who'd run the name through every database available and come back with the profile of a man who existed in the space between legitimate wealth and the kind of influence that didn't appear on tax returns. Sixty-one years old. Tech money, old money, money that had reproduced with other money until the resulting fortune had developed its own gravitational field. Board seats on three pharmaceutical companies, a defense contractor, and a private intelligence firm whose client list was classified at a level that made Kline's contacts uncomfortable.

Julian's voice came next, controlled, as always, but with an edge Lena hadn't heard before. Not anger. Constraint. The sound of a man holding something back with significant effort.

"This is not a product, Victor."

"Everything is a product. That's not cynicism. That's economics. You've built the most effective persuasion tool in human history, and you're using it to entertain rich people at dinner parties. Do you understand what this technology is worth?"

"It is not technology."

"It's a mechanism that reliably alters human behavior through auditory stimulus. That is, by any rational definition, technology. And technology scales."

"The Instrument does not scale. That is its nature. That is its limitation. That is, if you want to be precise about it, its safety feature."

"Its safety feature is that it doesn't work on enough people at once? Julian, I've spent forty million dollars funding this operation. I've been patient. I've been respectful. But patience has a maturity date, and we're past it."

Silence from behind the door. The particular silence of Julian Calder deciding what to say, which was different from the silence of Julian Calder deploying a pause. This one was heavier. Less certain.

A hand touched Lena's elbow. She turned to find Margaux Levine standing behind her in the corridor, close enough that their proximity felt deliberate. Margaux's face was pale. Not dramatically, not the pallor of illness or shock, but the subtle, systemic paleness of sustained anxiety, of cortisol doing its quiet, corrosive work on the capillaries.

"You heard?" Margaux said.

"Enough."

"He wants to scale it." Margaux's voice was barely above a whisper, but the urgency in it was louder than anything Victor Hale had said through the door. "Advertising. Political campaigns. Corporate training. He's been talking about it for months, but Julian kept blocking him. Now Victor's bringing in his own people, consultants, behavioral psychologists, media strategists, to study whether the cadence can be adapted for mass delivery."

"Can it?" Lena asked.

Margaux looked at her with the expression of a woman standing in a building she'd just realized was on fire. "I don't know. Nobody knows. That's the point. Julian has always insisted that the Instrument requires live delivery, proximity, precision. But Victor doesn't need it to work perfectly. He needs it to work well enough. At scale, even a degraded version, ten percent of the full effect, five percent, applied to millions of people through television, radio, podcast advertising..." She trailed off.

Lena finished the calculation silently. Even a partial effect, a mild increase in suggestibility, a subtle reduction in critical resistance, a barely perceptible shift in consumer behavior or political inclination, applied to an audience of millions would be worth more than forty million dollars. Worth more than any number Victor

Hale could imagine. Because the product wouldn't be the effect itself. The product would be the *deniability*. An influence mechanism that was invisible, undetectable, and, if the science remained obscure enough, indefensible in court.

"Does Julian know about the consultants?" Lena asked.

"He knows about some of them. Not all." Margaux glanced at Nadia, who was standing very still with her box of hard drives pressed against her chest like armor. "Nadia's been tracking Victor's parallel operation. Separate funding. Separate research team. Using fragments without Julian's oversight."

Lena looked at Nadia. The neuroscientist met her gaze with the steady, exhausted clarity of a woman who had been carrying too many secrets for too long and was reaching the point where the weight of them was either going to be shared or was going to crush her.

"Is that what I think it is?" Lena asked, nodding toward the box.

"Everything," Nadia said quietly. "All of it. Victor's research. Julian's research. My research. Listener data, brain scans, the full classification database. Every piece of evidence that what the Order does constitutes a measurable, reproducible alteration of human neurological function."

"You're leaking it."

Nadia's jaw tightened. "I'm preserving it. Victor wants to commercialize it. Julian wants to protect it. Both of them think they're right, and both of them are willing to destroy the evidence that proves the other one wrong." She looked at Lena directly. "You're the only person outside this organization with the expertise to understand what's in these files and the standing to do something about it. I'm choosing you."

Before Lena could respond, the door opened.

Victor Hale emerged first. He was exactly what his profile suggested: tall, silver-haired, impeccably dressed in the particular shade of charcoal that men who owned private jets wore when they wanted to project seriousness. His face was composed, but his jaw was tight, the residual tension of a man who had just been told no by someone who didn't have the money to say it.

He saw Lena and stopped. His eyes moved across her, not with the predatory assessment of a man evaluating a woman, but with the cooler, more clinical assessment of a man evaluating an asset. He recognized her. She could see it in the slight adjustment of his expression: the recalibration of a mind that was accustomed to knowing everything relevant about every person in every room it entered.

"Dr. Voss," he said. "I've been meaning to introduce myself."

"Mr. Hale."

He smiled. It was the kind of smile that had launched a thousand NDAs, warm, professional, and totally empty of warmth or professionalism. "I hope Julian has been hospitable. He can be quite persuasive when he wants to be." The emphasis on *persuasive* was subtle enough to be deniable and heavy enough to be unmistakable.

"He's been cooperative," Lena said.

"Cooperative." Victor tasted the word the way a sommelier tasted a wine he intended to send back. "I'm sure he has." He glanced at Nadia and the box in her arms, and something flickered behind his eyes, not suspicion, exactly, but the heightened attention of a man who made a habit of knowing what was in every box in every room.

"Research materials," Nadia said, before he could ask.

"Of course." Victor's smile didn't waver. "Well, Dr. Voss, I look forward to continuing this conversation. We have a great deal in common, you and I. We both understand that the value of a discovery depends entirely on how it's deployed."

He walked past them, down the corridor, through the foyer, out the front door, leaving behind the faint trace of expensive cologne and the distinct impression that the forty million dollars he'd invested in the Cadence Society had just, in his mind, been reclassified from "patronage" to "acquisition."

Julian appeared in the doorway.

He looked, for the first time since Lena had met him, tired. Not physically, his posture was as controlled as ever, his clothing as precise, his eyes as attentive. But beneath the surface architecture of his composure, there was a fatigue that hadn't been there before. The fatigue of a man who had been holding something together for a long time and was beginning to feel the structural integrity of his grip approaching its limits.

He looked at Lena. At Nadia. At the box.

He said nothing.

But the look he gave Nadia, the brief, unguarded, unbearably human look of a man watching someone he trusted make a choice he couldn't control, told Lena everything she needed to know about the state of the Cadence Society.

It was breaking.

And the pieces, when they fell, would be sharp enough to cut everyone standing nearby.

• • •

CHAPTER FOURTEEN: *The Performer Breaks*

The call came from Margaux, and the sound of her voice was wrong.

Not wrong in the way that Lena had become accustomed to diagnosing, no cadence manipulation, no rhythmic distortion, no embedded patterns reaching through the phone for her respiratory system. Wrong in a simpler, more human way. Margaux sounded like a woman who had been crying hard enough to reshape the musculature of her throat, and who was now trying to speak through the wreckage.

"Something happened," Margaux said. "At a private session. Victor's people. I need, can you come?"

Lena was in a cab within four minutes.

The address was a townhouse in Gramercy, one of Victor Hale's properties, according to the quick text exchange she'd had with Kline while the cab navigated crosstown traffic. Kline was on his way. He'd arrive in twenty minutes. She didn't wait.

The door was answered by a man in a dark suit who had the build and the blankness of private security. He assessed her without interest and stepped aside, which told her that someone had authorized her entry in advance. Margaux, probably. Or Victor, hedging his bets.

The ground floor was in the particular disarray of a social event that had ended badly. Wine glasses on surfaces. Chairs pushed back. A cluster of people near the far wall, some seated, some standing, all of them wearing the shell-shocked expressions of civilians who had just been in proximity to something they didn't have the framework to process. In the center of the room, a paramedic was kneeling beside a man in his fifties who lay on his side on the carpet, conscious but disoriented, an oxygen mask covering his nose and mouth.

Margaux was sitting on a staircase to the left, arms wrapped around her knees, a blanket draped over her shoulders despite the warmth of the room. She looked up when Lena entered, and the expression on her face was the expression of a bridge that had just discovered it had been carrying more weight than its specifications allowed.

Lena went to her first.

"Tell me what happened."

Margaux's breathing was irregular, not patterned, not entrained, just broken. The breathing of a woman whose body had forgotten its rhythm and hadn't yet found a new one.

"Victor set up a private demonstration," she said. "For investors. Eight people. He wanted me to perform the full preparatory sequence, the same material I do at the salons, and then transition into the first quatrain of the Instrument."

"The first four lines."

"Yes. It's a standard practice performance. Build the room's entrainment through the prep material, then introduce the sonnet fragment once the audience is primed. Julian and I have done it dozens of times. It's controlled. It's safe."

"But Julian wasn't here."

Margaux shook her head. "Victor insisted on running it without him. Said he needed proof that the effect was reproducible without Julian's personal involvement. Independent demonstration."

Lena filed that, Victor wasn't just trying to commercialize the sonnet. He was trying to prove that

Julian was unnecessary. That the mechanism could be separated from its master practitioner and handed to anyone with sufficient training.

"So you performed alone."

"I've performed alone before. Not often, but I can do it. The prep material is mine, I wrote it based on the sonnet's rhythmic profile. I know it. I've delivered it a hundred times." She paused, and something in her face crumbled, not completely, but enough to show the foundation. "But tonight was different."

"Different how?"

Margaux's hands tightened around her knees. "The room was wrong. Victor's acoustic setup was cheap, commercial sound panels, basic dampening, nothing like Julian's precision engineering. The resonance profile was uneven. There were dead spots and hot spots and the low-frequency feedback was all wrong. I compensated, I've been trained to adjust for imperfect acoustics, but the compensation changed my delivery. I was pushing harder than usual. Using more breath pressure. More volume. More force."

Lena could see where this was going. The mechanism was delicate, Julian had said so repeatedly. Precision was not a luxury; it was a safety requirement. Modify the delivery parameters even slightly and the effect changed. Push too hard and the smooth, escalating cascade of parasympathetic compliance could tip into something else, something the body interpreted not as an invitation to surrender but as an assault.

"What happened when you started the quatrain?"

Margaux closed her eyes. "It was fine at first. The standard response, breathing synchronization, postural softening, the usual. Seven of the eight listeners were tracking normally. But the eighth, the man on the floor, he wasn't responding the way the others were. His breathing was syncing, but his heart rate was going up instead of down. I could see it in his face. He was tightening, not opening."

"Sympathetic activation instead of parasympathetic."

"Yes. And I should have stopped. I should have recognized it and pulled back and broken the cadence. That's what Julian would have done. That's what I was trained to do." Margaux's voice fractured on the word *trained,* splitting along a fault line that had probably been widening for years. "But I didn't stop. Because the cadence was pulling *me.*"

Lena went still.

"I was three lines into the quatrain," Margaux continued, "and I could feel it. Not just delivering it, *receiving* it. The words were coming out of my mouth and going into the room and coming back to me through the acoustics, and the feedback loop was, it was like singing in a cathedral, except the cathedral was singing back. My own delivery was entraining my own nervous system."

"A feedback loop," Lena said. "The performer becomes the listener."

"Yes. And once it started, I couldn't, I tried to pull back, tried to change the cadence, tried to break the rhythm, and I *couldn't.* My body wouldn't let me. It had locked onto the pattern and the pattern was coming from *me* and I couldn't stop producing it without stopping speaking and I couldn't stop speaking because—"

She stopped. Her breathing hitched. For a long, terrible moment, Margaux Levine sat on the staircase of Victor Hale's townhouse and fought a battle with her own diaphragm that was written across her face in the language of genuine, unperformable distress.

"Because it felt too good to stop," she finished, so quietly that Lena had to lean in to hear it.

Lena sat with that for a moment. Then: "What broke it?"

"The man seized. The one whose heart rate was climbing. He made a sound, this horrible, strangled noise, and it was irregular enough to shatter the cadence. The feedback loop broke. I stopped speaking. And then I just..." She gestured vaguely at herself, at the blanket, at the wreckage of the evening. "Fell."

Lena looked across the room at the man on the floor. The paramedic was checking his pupils. His vitals appeared stable, the seizure had been brief, triggered not by the sonnet's intended effect but by its unintended one, the sympathetic overload of a nervous system that had been pushed into fight-or-flight by an acoustic assault it had no defense against.

"Margaux," Lena said. "How long have you been performing for the Order?"

"Three years."

"And in those three years, have you ever experienced the feedback effect before?"

Margaux was quiet for a long time. Long enough that the silence became its own answer.

"Not like tonight," she said finally. "Not that strong. But... yes. Small moments. During salon performances, when the room's entrainment is high and the acoustics are right, there are moments where I feel the cadence pulling at me. I've always been able to manage it. Compartmentalize it. Treat it as a known variable and adjust."

She looked up at Lena, and what was in her eyes was not the composed, magnetic beauty of the woman who had commanded a room full of thirty listeners at the salon. It was the raw, undecorated terror of someone who had just realized that the instrument they'd been playing had been playing them back.

"It's been eating me alive," she said. "For three years, and I didn't know until the floor dropped out. Every performance, a little more. Every delivery, a little deeper. And I thought I was in control because I was the one speaking, but I wasn't. I was just the delivery mechanism. And delivery mechanisms don't get to decide what they carry."

Lena reached out and took Margaux's hand. It was not a clinical gesture. It was not a professional gesture. It was the gesture of one woman recognizing another's terror because she carried a version of it herself, smaller, differently shaped, but cut from the same cloth.

"You're done performing," Lena said. "Starting now."

Margaux's fingers tightened around hers. "Julian won't—"

"Julian doesn't get a vote." Lena held her gaze. "The sonnet consumes its speakers too. You just proved that. And if it's been accumulating for three years, then every performance you give from this point forward increases the risk that the feedback loop catches you permanently."

She didn't say *like Daniel Mercer*. She didn't need to.

Margaux understood.

The tears came then, quiet, controlled, the tears of a woman who had trained herself to perform even grief with precision. But the relief beneath them was real. The relief of someone who had been given permission to stop carrying something they'd been told was an honor but had always suspected was a sentence.

Kline arrived twelve minutes later. By then, the man on the floor was conscious and coherent, the other guests had been escorted out, and Victor Hale's security team had positioned themselves at every exit with the professional nonchalance of people who were very good at preventing things from leaving buildings.

Kline surveyed the scene with the expression of a man who was adding items to a very long list.

"Charges?" he asked Lena, quietly.

"Not yet. But soon."

He nodded. Looked at Margaux on the staircase, at the blanket around her shoulders, at the tear-streaked face of a woman who had just learned the true cost of the instrument she'd been given.

"Another victim?" he asked.

Lena looked at Margaux. At the woman who had spent three years being consumed by the thing she carried. Who had believed she was an artist when she was, in fact, a conduit. Who had felt the beauty of the sonnet flowing through her and hadn't realized that beauty, like radiation, could be lethal at sufficient exposure.

"Yes," Lena said. "Another victim."

• • •

CHAPTER FIFTEEN: *Harris Unravels*

Harris Cole had stopped sleeping.

Lena knew this because she'd been monitoring him, not through any official program, but through the informal arrangement she'd established with the university counseling center after flagging him as a person of concern during the investigation. Weekly check-ins. Voluntary. Harris had agreed to them with the eager compliance of a young man who wanted desperately to believe that what was happening to him was manageable.

It was not manageable.

She found him in a study room on the fourth floor of Butler Library, surrounded by books he wasn't reading. His laptop was open to a word processor document filled with text that, at a distance, looked like notes but at closer range revealed itself to be something else: lines and fragments arranged and rearranged in different configurations, each permutation separated by a blank line, each sequence a slightly different attempt to recreate something from memory that wouldn't quite resolve into clarity.

He was trying to reconstruct the words his lips had spoken without his permission in the interview room. The phrase he'd completed. The sentence that had ended with *obeys*.

"Harris," Lena said from the doorway.

He startled. Not the reflexive startle of someone surprised, the full-body jolt of someone whose nervous system was running on cortisol and insufficient rest, a system wound so tight that any stimulus registered as threat before it registered as information.

"Dr. Voss." He minimized the document with the practiced speed of someone who'd been caught before. Not by her. By himself. By the part of his mind that knew what he was doing was wrong, or at least unwise, and couldn't stop doing it anyway.

"When did you last sleep?" she asked, sitting across from him.

"Last night."

His eyes told a different story. The sclera were bloodshot, the skin beneath puffy and darkened, the pupils slightly dilated with the adrenergic load of sustained sleep deprivation. He'd been awake for at least thirty-six hours, probably longer.

"Harris."

He looked away. "Two days. Maybe three. I lose track."

"Because of the rhythm."

He flinched at the word. Not dramatically, a micro-flinch, the kind that most people would miss. But Lena had been watching for it, because she knew what it meant. The word *rhythm* had become a trigger. Not the kind of trigger that produced panic or flashback, the kind that produced *craving*. The word activated the same neural pathways that the sonnet fragments had begun to carve into his auditory processing centers, and each activation reinforced the pathways, and each reinforcement made the craving slightly stronger, slightly more insistent, slightly harder to ignore.

"It's always there," Harris said. "In the background. Like a song stuck in your head, except it's not a song. It's more like... a shape. A shape that my brain keeps trying to fill in. And every time I almost hear it, in traffic noise, in the rhythm of someone talking, in the pattern of my own heartbeat, my body reacts. My breathing changes. My chest gets warm. And then it fades, and the fading is—"

He stopped. Swallowed.

"The fading is worse than not hearing it at all," he finished.

Lena recognized the description with the clinical precision of her training and the visceral understanding of her own experience. Harris was describing the anticipation loop, the neurological craving generated by partial exposure to a pattern that demanded completion. His brain had received enough of the sonnet's rhythmic structure to predict what came next, and each time the prediction went unfulfilled, the gap between expectation and reality produced a neurochemical deficit that his body experienced as need.

It was, in the most precise neurological sense, the same mechanism that drove addiction. Not chemical addiction, structural addiction. His neural architecture had been remodeled to expect a stimulus that wasn't coming, and the absence of that stimulus was, to his brain, indistinguishable from withdrawal.

"I've been trying the techniques you taught me," he said. "The irregular breathing. The pattern disruption. They help. For a while. But the relief doesn't last. It's like holding your breath underwater, you can do it, but eventually your body takes over."

Lena nodded. She'd expected this. The techniques she'd given him were designed for acute pattern disruption, breaking the entrainment in real time, snapping the listener out of synchronization. They were not designed for chronic exposure effects, because chronic exposure effects required a different intervention entirely, one that she hadn't yet figured out how to provide.

"Have you been seeking out the fragments?" she asked. She kept her voice neutral, non-judgmental. The question was clinical. The implications were not.

Harris's gaze dropped to the table. To the laptop he'd minimized. To the document full of rearranged words that he'd been working on when she arrived.

"Yes," he said.

"What have you found?"

"Nothing that works. Nothing that matches. I've tried reading poetry, Shakespeare, other Elizabethan verse, modern sonnets, anything with iambic pentameter, hoping that something would scratch the itch. Nothing does. It's not the meter. It's something more specific. A particular combination of stress and pause and phonetic shape that I can almost hear but never quite—"

He stopped again. His breathing had changed, faster, shallower, the respiratory signature of someone approaching the edge of a craving that their body wanted to fall into.

Lena watched him struggle and felt the weight of her expertise press down on her like a physical thing. She knew what would help him. She knew that the craving was generated by incompleteness and that the cure for incompleteness was completion. She knew that if Harris heard the full sonnet, the real one, delivered with precision, allowed to run its course, the anticipation loop would resolve. The craving would subside. The neural pathways that were screaming for resolution would receive what they'd been demanding, and the neurochemical deficit would fill.

She also knew what would happen after that.

Completion wasn't relief. Completion was capture. Harris would feel better, temporarily, profoundly, with the full-body satisfaction of a craving finally met, and then the satisfaction would fade, and what would remain in its place would be not the craving for completion but the craving for *repetition*. He would want to hear it again. And again. And the interval between wanting and needing would shorten with each exposure until the distinction between the two disappeared entirely, and Harris Cole would join Daniel Mercer in the quiet, perfect, eternal stillness of a mind that had stopped needing anything the world could provide.

"Dr. Voss," Harris said, and his voice had changed. Quieter now. More focused. The voice of a man who had arrived at a request he'd been circling for weeks and had finally decided to land on it. "I need to ask you something."

"Go ahead."

"You have the fragments. I know you do. The ones from Dr. Ashcroft's research. The ones you've been studying." He looked up at her, and his eyes carried the particular desperate clarity of someone who had exhausted every alternative and was left with the one option they'd been told to avoid. "Let me hear it. The real thing. Once. All the way through. If the pattern completes, the craving will stop."

Lena held his gaze and said nothing.

"I know what you're going to say," he continued. "You're going to say it'll make things worse. That completion leads to dependency. That I'll end up like that man, the one in the facility. I know the theory. But Dr. Voss, the theory is *abstract,* and what I'm living with is not abstract. It's every second of every day. It's the sound of my own heartbeat trying to match a rhythm I can barely remember. It's lying awake at three in the morning feeling like my body is waiting for permission to do something and I don't know what the something is. I am falling apart one unfinished bar of music at a time."

The words landed in the study room with the weight of something that had been carried too long and set down too hard. Harris's eyes were wet. Not with tears, with the glassy sheen of exhaustion and desperation and the specific kind of honesty that only emerged when all the more comfortable alternatives had been used up.

Lena looked at this young man, twenty-four years old, brilliant, ambitious, who had walked into his advisor's office to drop off revisions and had walked out with a neurological wound that was slowly, quietly, relentlessly widening, and she felt two things at once.

Compassion. Deep, genuine, uncomplicated compassion for a human being in pain.

And understanding. The specific, terrible, personal understanding of someone who knew exactly what the craving felt like because she had felt it herself, in the evidence lab, in her office, at the salon, in every quiet moment when the rhythm crept back into her consciousness like a tide returning to a shore it would never stop visiting.

She understood his logic. She understood the seductive clarity of it, *if it finishes, it stops*. She understood because a part of her, small but persistent, had been making the same argument every night when she lay in bed and felt the unfinished pattern turning in the back of her mind like a key in a lock that hadn't quite caught.

"I can't do that, Harris," she said.

His face didn't collapse. It solidified. The hope draining out and the resignation setting in, not like water leaving a vessel but like concrete pouring into one.

"Then what?" he asked.

"I'm working on something," she said. "A disruption protocol. Not just acute, structural. Something that can address the chronic craving without completing the pattern."

"How long?"

"I don't know."

"And in the meantime?"

Lena reached across the table and placed her hand over his. His skin was cold, slightly clammy, the peripheral vasoconstriction of a body running on stress hormones and not much else.

"In the meantime," she said, "you call me. Any time. Day or night. When the craving peaks, you call me and we work through it together. You are not alone in this, Harris. I need you to hear that."

He looked at her hand on his. Then at her face. And in his eyes, beneath the exhaustion and the craving and the quiet disintegration of a life that had been interrupted by something it was never designed to encounter, she saw something she recognized.

Gratitude. Not for the answer, the answer hadn't been what he wanted. Gratitude for the honesty. For being treated as a person rather than a data point. For the simple, enormous act of someone saying *you are not alone* and meaning it.

"Okay," he said.

"Okay."

She squeezed his hand once and released it. Stood. Gathered her coat.

At the door, she turned back.

Harris was looking at his laptop again. At the minimized document. At the rearranged fragments of a pattern that his mind couldn't stop chasing.

She wanted to tell him to close it. To delete it. To stop looking for something that would destroy him if he found it.

But she didn't. Because she had a drawer in her own desk that contained the same kind of fragments, arranged with the same kind of desperate precision, locked away with the same key that she kept in her pocket at all times because she didn't trust herself not to open the drawer if the key was anywhere she could reach it easily.

She left the library and walked into the November night and did not call Kline, because what she was feeling was not something that could be shared with a man whose resistance was constitutional rather than earned.

Instead, she walked. Twelve blocks in the cold, breathing hard, breathing deliberately, breathing in patterns that belonged to no one but herself.

And tried not to think about how well she understood Harris Cole's request.

And how close she was to making the same one.

• • •

CHAPTER SIXTEEN: *The Night She Listened*

She told herself it was research.

That was the first lie, and it was a good one, well-constructed, internally consistent, and supported by a foundation of professional obligation that could bear the weight of almost any rationalization. She needed to understand the full architecture of the sonnet. She needed to map the complete rhythmic cascade, from first line to last, in order to develop the structural disruption protocol she'd promised Harris. She needed the data that only firsthand exposure could provide.

All true. All reasonable. All cover.

It was eleven-forty on a Tuesday night, and Lena was alone in her office with the door locked and the lights low and the near-complete text of Sonnet 155 laid out on her desk like a patient on an operating table.

She'd assembled it over the past week from Ashcroft's fragments, Julian's archive, Nadia's research files, and her own analysis. Twelve lines. The first three quatrains, meticulously reconstructed. The final couplet remained missing, or rather, she had one version of it, taken from Daniel Mercer's lips, but she wasn't certain it was accurate. The couplet was the resolution. The payoff. The place where the pattern completed itself. And the pattern, she suspected, was very specific about how it wanted to be completed.

So she had twelve lines. Not fourteen. Twelve.

That's safe, she told herself. *The effect requires completion. Without the couplet, the cascade can't resolve. You'll feel the build, observe the mechanism, document the progression, and stop. Like a controlled burn. Like a stress test. Like any other experiment you've ever conducted on a phenomenon you needed to understand.*

The second lie was the metronome.

She'd brought it. It sat on the corner of the desk, loaded and ready, its digital display showing 92 bpm, the same off-sync tempo she'd used before, the same rhythmic countermeasure that had anchored her breathing during her last solo exposure. She'd placed it there with the same deliberate, visible intention with which a recovering alcoholic might place a glass of water beside a bottle of wine, a signal to herself that she was in control, that she had safeguards, that the distance between observation and surrender was being actively maintained.

She didn't turn it on.

That was when the lying stopped and the truth began.

Lena sat in her chair, the twelve lines in front of her, the metronome dark and silent beside her, and she acknowledged, quietly, privately, in the space between her breath and the next, that she was not here to research.

She was here to feel it again.

The warmth. The resonance. The exquisite, terrifying precision of a pattern that knew the exact frequency at which her nervous system operated and was offering to match it, to synchronize with it, to create the specific form of harmony that her body craved with an intensity that no professional obligation or personal discipline had been able to suppress.

She wanted it. Not intellectually. Not clinically. With her body. With the animal, autonomic, pre-rational architecture of a nervous system that had been offered perfection and told no, and that had spent every moment since then remembering what perfection tasted like.

She picked up the page.

Read the first line.

Aloud.

"When breath is lent to shape the yielding ear..."

The words left her mouth and entered the room, and the room changed. Not physically, the walls didn't move, the light didn't shift, the temperature didn't alter. But the acoustic quality of the space transformed, the way a theater transformed when the first line of a play was spoken: from a room containing objects to a space containing intention. Her voice, speaking these words in this rhythm, gave the room a pulse. And the pulse was not the room's.

It was hers.

Her breathing adjusted on the first line. Not violently, not dramatically, a gentle, involuntary recalibration, her diaphragm expanding to accommodate a rhythm that the words were suggesting without demanding. She noticed the adjustment and did not correct it.

That was the third lie. The one she told herself in real time: *I'm observing the effect. I need to let it engage in order to study it. Correcting now would compromise the data.*

"And cadence binds what reason would defy..."

Her chest warmed. The same warmth she'd felt before, in the evidence lab, at the salon, in Julian's performance room, but deeper now, fuller, the warmth of a body that had been primed by multiple partial exposures and was responding to the current stimulus with the accumulated sensitivity of every exposure that had come before. Julian had warned her about this. Each encounter lowered the threshold. Each fragment made the next encounter more potent.

She'd known that.

She was doing it anyway.

"The pulse forgets the boundary of fear, and learns at last the sweetness of comply..."

The first quatrain completed, and the resolution hit her like a wave, not the crashing, violent kind, but the deep, slow, oceanic kind that lifted everything in its path without disturbing anything on the surface. The word *comply* landed on a stressed syllable after a sequence of unstressed ones, and her brain processed the resolution as a reward: a micro-burst of dopamine, a flush of endorphin, a neurochemical kiss that said *yes, good, continue, more.*

She continued.

"Let not the tongue declare what mind resists, for softer chains are forged in tempered sound..."

Her shoulders dropped. Not fractionally, not tentatively, *completely*. Every stored tension in her trapezius muscles released at once, the way a fist unclenched after being held too long, and the release felt so good that she inhaled sharply at the pleasure of it, which was a mistake, because the sharp inhale broke her rhythm for half a second and then the rhythm recaptured her with a gentleness that was worse than force.

"A silken tyranny through silence twists, till will lies still, yet pleasure is unbound..."

She was speaking more slowly now. Not because she was reading carefully. Because her body was savoring it. Each word was a piece of something being assembled inside her, and she could feel the architecture forming, not in her mind, which remained alert, observant, documenting everything with the dispassionate precision of a researcher even as her body abandoned its professional obligations entirely, but in her nervous system, where something old and deep and patient was settling into place with the quiet satisfaction of a key entering a lock it had been designed for.

"What art is this, that humbles crown and creed..."

Her eyes were half-closed. When had that happened? She couldn't remember the moment of transition, couldn't pinpoint the instant when her eyelids had decided, independently of her conscious intention, to lower themselves into the posture of reception, of surrender, of a body that wanted to feel more and see less.

"And bends the spine without a hand or blade..."

Her spine curved. Forward. Not collapse, *yield.* The word *bends* in the line was an instruction that her body executed before her mind could intercept it, and the execution felt not like obedience but like agreement, like her skeleton had been holding a shape it didn't want and was finally being given permission to assume the one it preferred.

"A whispered law no sovereign can impede, where flesh obeys, though thought would barricade..."

Twelve lines. Three quatrains. The end of what she had.

The pattern reached forward. Into the space where the couplet should have been. Into the silence that followed the twelfth line, a silence that was not empty but *aching,* vibrating with the specific, unbearable tension of an unresolved chord, a sentence without a period, a breath drawn in with no exhale to follow.

Her body wanted the couplet.

Not wanted, *needed.* The distinction had dissolved somewhere around line eight, somewhere in the warm, deep, exquisite cascade of a nervous system operating in perfect synchronization with an external rhythm that knew it better than it knew itself. The need was physical. Present. Undeniable. A pressure in her chest, a fullness in her lungs, a trembling in the muscles of her jaw that wasn't cold or fear but the vibration of a string that had been tuned to a frequency and then denied the note that would make it sing.

She knew the couplet. She had Daniel Mercer's version, transcribed from his silent lips. She could speak it. She could complete the pattern. She could let the architecture finish itself and experience the resolution that twelve lines of escalating perfection had been building toward with the inexorable momentum of gravity.

All she had to do was continue.

Two more lines.

Fourteen words.

The end.

Lena Marchetti sat in her office, breathing in iambic pentameter, every muscle in her body softened to the point of dissolution, her nervous system alight with the warm, precise, devastating pleasure of a pattern that had been waiting four hundred years for someone who could feel it this completely, and she stopped.

The effort was physical.

Not metaphorical. Not cognitive. *Physical.* Her diaphragm clenched. Her jaw locked. Her hands, which had been resting open in her lap, when had she opened her hands?, closed into fists, fingernails pressing into palms, the sharp bite of pain a wedge driven between the pattern's momentum and her body's willingness to follow it.

She forced an exhale. Wrong rhythm. Wrong timing. Ugly. Broken. The anti-cadence of a woman dismantling something beautiful because the beauty was a trap.

The pattern shattered.

The warmth didn't fade. It *recoiled*, pulling back from her extremities like a tide reversing, leaving in its wake a cold that felt disproportionate to the room temperature, a hollowness in her chest where the resonance had been, a sudden, vertiginous sense of loss that made her grip the edge of the desk and hold on while the room stopped spinning.

She sat in the dark.

Breathing.

Ragged. Irregular. Her own.

Her heart hammered. Not from fear. From something worse: from the physiological aftermath of having been very, very close to something her body had desperately wanted and having denied it at the last possible moment. The neurochemistry of interrupted climax. The specific, punishing withdrawal of a brain that had been promised resolution and received instead a wall.

Minutes passed. She didn't count them. She breathed and she held the desk and she waited for her nervous system to remember that it belonged to her and not to a pattern of syllables on a piece of paper.

When she could think again, really think, not just observe herself from inside the fog, she acknowledged what she'd been denying since the first night in her apartment, since the humming, since the salon, since the moment in the evidence lab when her lungs had adjusted to a line carved in wood by a dead man's unknown visitor.

She was not Resistant.

She was Receptive.

Highly Receptive. Profoundly Receptive. Possibly, and this was the part that made her want to laugh, or cry, or both, the most Receptive person who had ever encountered this particular arrangement of syllables.

Julian had said as much. She'd filed it away as his professional opinion. She'd treated it as a data point, an observation about her neurological profile that was interesting but manageable.

It was not manageable.

It was the defining fact of her relationship with the sonnet, and it meant that everything she'd believed about herself, every firewall, every defense, every carefully constructed boundary between the woman who studied influence and the woman who was influenced, was thinner than she'd known. Not absent. Not destroyed. But thin. And getting thinner with every exposure.

She looked at the page on her desk. Twelve lines, face-up, still vibrating with the residual potential of everything they had almost done.

She turned it over.

Then she pulled the metronome toward her and turned it on. 92 bpm. Steady, indifferent, mechanical. The most unromantic sound in the world.

She sat with it for a long time.

And in the cold, broken, ruthlessly honest space that the metronome's ticking carved out of the silence, she admitted the last thing.

She wanted to hear the end.

Not because she needed to understand it. Not because her research demanded it. Not because Harris was suffering and the disruption protocol required data and the investigation needed evidence.

She wanted to hear the end because the sonnet had offered her something she hadn't known she was looking for, the experience of every cell in her body operating in perfect alignment with something outside herself, and she wanted it again.

And again.

And again.

She turned off the lamp. Left the page face-down on the desk. Gathered her coat.

Walked out of the building into the November dark, where the wind was irregular and the traffic was chaotic and nothing, nothing, nothing in the world was in iambic pentameter except the traitorous, persistent, impossibly beautiful rhythm that played behind her eyes with every step she took toward home.

• • •

CHAPTER SEVENTEEN: *The Betrayal*

Nadia Osei had been planning her exit for six weeks, and she was twenty minutes away from completing it when Julian found her.

The archive room was in the sub-basement of his building, a climate-controlled vault with steel shelving and filtered air and the particular silence of a space designed to protect things that were old and dangerous from things that were new and careless. Nadia had access. She'd always had access. That was the problem with being the Order's researcher: you knew where everything was kept, you understood what everything meant, and when you decided that the people keeping it couldn't be trusted with it anymore, you had a very efficient head start.

She was copying the last of the historical files, the original marginalia records, the 18th-century correspondence between Order members that documented the first deliberate fragmentation of the sonnet, the handwritten analysis by a man named Aldous Bell who had been, as far as anyone could determine, the first person to understand why the complete text was dangerous, when the door opened behind her and Julian's voice entered the room before he did.

"Nadia."

Just her name. Spoken in his natural register, without cadence manipulation, without the deliberate architecture of the Instrument. But his natural voice still carried the resonance of a man who had spent twenty-three years training it, and even stripped of technique, it filled the room with an authority that was less a choice than a condition.

She didn't stop copying. "I'm backing up the archive. Routine maintenance."

"You're duplicating the Aldous Bell correspondence for Dr. Voss."

She stopped. Not because he'd caught her, she'd known the risk, accepted it, factored it into her timeline. She stopped because the sound of Lena's name in Julian's mouth carried a weight that wasn't professional, wasn't strategic, wasn't part of the careful, constructed personality he presented to the world. It was personal. And personal from Julian was a tectonic event.

"Yes," Nadia said. She turned to face him. "I am."

Julian stood in the doorway with his hands at his sides and an expression that was, for him, extraordinarily naked. Not angry. Not betrayed. Tired. The bone-deep tiredness of a man who had been holding a position for a very long time and was beginning to feel the structural fatigue in places he couldn't reinforce.

"You understand what you're doing," he said.

"I understand exactly what I'm doing. I'm giving the foremost expert on neurolinguistic manipulation access to the complete historical record of the most significant neurolinguistic phenomenon ever documented. I am, in other words, doing what a scientist is supposed to do when her institution has failed to self-regulate."

The words were steady. She'd rehearsed them. Not because she was afraid of Julian, she'd worked beside him for eight years, and fear was not what she felt, but because she knew that Julian's gift was his ability to reshape conversations in real time, and the only defense against a reshaping was to have your own shape fixed before you entered the room.

Julian closed the door behind him. The click of the latch had the specific, sobering quality of a conversation that had just become private.

"Victor's funding is compromised," he said. "His parallel research program has been using fragments without adequate safety protocols. Two people are dead. Three more are showing symptoms consistent with early-stage entrainment. I know all of this, Nadia. I've known it for longer than you think."

"Then why haven't you stopped it?"

The question filled the room the way water fills a glass, completely, immediately, leaving no space for anything else.

Julian was quiet for a long time.

"Because stopping Victor means exposing the Order," he said. "And exposing the Order means exposing the Instrument. And exposing the Instrument means—"

"Letting other people decide what to do with it," Nadia finished. "Yes. That's the part that scares you."

"It should scare you too."

"It does. But it scares me less than watching you and Victor fight over custody of something that neither of you should be parenting." She took a step toward him, and the step carried more than distance, it carried eight years of observation, eight years of watching a brilliant man make increasingly narrow decisions in service of something he called preservation and she had begun to call ownership. "Julian, you can't keep it. You never could. The Instrument isn't a possession. It's a phenomenon. And phenomena don't belong to the people who discover them. They belong to the world."

Julian's jaw tightened. "The world is not equipped to handle it."

"The world handled fire. The world handled nuclear fission. The world handles every dangerous discovery by arguing about it, regulating it, occasionally misusing it, and eventually incorporating it into the species' collective understanding of what's possible. That's how progress works. It's messy and it's dangerous and it's the only process that actually functions."

"Fire didn't require a willing listener. Nuclear fission didn't amplify the listener's own desires and use them as the mechanism of control. The Instrument is—"

"Is what?" Nadia's voice sharpened. Not with anger, with the precision of a scientist who had heard the argument before and was no longer willing to let it stand unchallenged. "Different? Special? Too dangerous for ordinary minds? Julian, that's the argument that every custodian of every dangerous secret has ever made, and it's always wrong, and it's always self-serving, and it always ends the same way: with the secret getting out anyway, but later and worse, because the custodians spent so much time protecting it that they never developed the safeguards that public scrutiny would have demanded."

The silence that followed was the most honest sound Lena would ever hear described to her by the two people who had been in the room when it happened. Nadia would tell her about it the next day, sitting in Lena's office with the copied files in a box at her feet, her voice steady and her eyes carrying the particular weight of a woman who had just blown up the most important professional relationship of her life and was still deciding whether to grieve or celebrate.

"He stood there," Nadia would say, "and I watched the argument die in his face. Not because I'd convinced him. Because he'd already convinced himself, somewhere underneath all that composure, and my saying it out loud just made it impossible to pretend otherwise."

But that was the next day. In the moment, in the vault, Julian Calder looked at the woman who had been his most trusted researcher for eight years and who was now, with deliberate and irreversible intent, dismantling the architecture of secrecy he had spent his entire adult life constructing.

And he said something that Nadia had not expected.

"You're building a cathedral you'll never pray in."

It took her a moment. The phrase was her own, she'd said it to him weeks ago, in a different context, about his relationship to the sonnet. About his inability to experience its effects. About the tragic, defining irony of a man who had perfected an art he could never personally enter.

He was throwing it back at her. But not as an attack. As a mirror.

"You believe that exposing the Instrument will lead to understanding," he said. "To regulation. To the kind of rational, democratic process that eventually tames every dangerous discovery. But you will never experience what it does, Nadia. Not because you're Resistant, because you refuse to. You've spent eight years studying it from the outside, documenting its effects on other people, measuring what it does to nervous systems that aren't yours. You have built a cathedral of data about something you've never felt."

"That's called science, Julian."

"No," he said. "That's called safety. And I don't begrudge you it. But don't stand in my archive and tell me that the world is ready for something you yourself won't touch."

The accusation landed, and Nadia felt it. Not because it was true, or not entirely, but because it was the kind of truth that Julian Calder specialized in: the kind that was accurate enough to wound and selective enough to mislead.

"The difference between us," she said, "is that I know I'm afraid of it. You've convinced yourself you're above it. And that's more dangerous than anything in this vault."

Julian's composure cracked.

Not dramatically. Not with the visible fracturing of a mask that broke cleanly along its fault lines. More like a tremor, a seismic event that registered on the surface as a slight trembling of the hands, a barely perceptible tightening of the muscles around his eyes, a single, sharp breath that was the first uncontrolled breath Nadia had ever heard him take.

It lasted two seconds.

Then the composure reassembled, seamlessly, as though the tremor had been absorbed by a structure designed to withstand exactly this kind of stress.

"That," he said quietly, "is exactly why it must be perfect."

Nadia stared at him. And in the silence that followed, she understood something about Julian Calder that she had suspected but never confirmed.

He wasn't protecting the Instrument because he believed the world wasn't ready.

He was perfecting the Instrument because he believed that if he made it perfect enough, precise enough, controlled enough, beautiful enough, it would finally work on him.

The man who couldn't feel the sonnet had spent his entire life refining it, not for the listeners, not for the Order, not for posterity.

For himself.

In the desperate, unspoken, unacknowledged hope that one day, the thing he'd made would be good enough to reach even the one mind it had always failed to touch.

His own.

Nadia picked up the box of copied files.

"I'm sorry, Julian," she said. And meant it.

He stepped aside and let her pass.

The door closed between them, and the vault returned to its climate-controlled silence, and Julian Calder stood alone among the carefully preserved records of a phenomenon he had dedicated his life to perfecting and would never, in all the years remaining to him, personally understand.

• • •

CHAPTER EIGHTEEN: *The Deal*

Victor Hale moved on a Thursday.

Lena learned about it from Nadia, who called at seven in the morning with the clipped efficiency of a woman delivering intelligence rather than making conversation. Victor had engaged three independent practitioners, not Order-trained, not Julian-approved, but private vocal coaches and behavioral psychologists who'd been given enough of the theoretical framework to attempt a working delivery. He'd booked a venue: a converted warehouse in the Meatpacking District, the kind of industrial chic space that Manhattan's investor class used for product launches and TED-style presentations when they wanted the aesthetics of disruption without the inconvenience of actual change.

The event was scheduled for Saturday evening. Fifty guests. Private security. No phones permitted inside. The guest list, which Nadia had obtained through means Lena chose not to investigate, read like a who's who of people who shaped the world's economy from positions that didn't require name tags: venture capital partners, pharmaceutical executives, media conglomerate board members, and two people whose names Lena recognized from foreign policy briefings Kline had shown her during a previous case.

Victor wasn't just demonstrating the sonnet. He was pitching it.

"If those practitioners attempt a full delivery without Julian's precision," Nadia said, "the effect will be unstable. Imprecise. We saw what happened at the Gramercy session with Margaux, and she was trained.

These people aren't. They'll be using the mechanism like a blunt instrument."

"And in a room of fifty people," Lena said, "at least some of them will be Resistant. The effect will hit different people differently. Some will comply. Some will panic. Some—"

"Some will have the same cardiac response as Ashcroft."

Lena closed her eyes. "People will die."

"Yes."

The simplicity of the confirmation sat in the morning air like a verdict. Not a possibility. A certainty. The mechanism was precise enough to kill when deployed imprecisely, Ashcroft's death had proven that, and Priya Dasgupta's had confirmed it. A room of fifty people subjected to an uncontrolled delivery by practitioners who didn't fully understand the instrument they were wielding was not a demonstration. It was a mass casualty event wearing a cocktail dress.

"I can't stop this alone," Lena said.

Nadia was quiet for a moment. Then: "No. You can't."

"And the police?"

"What would you tell them? That a poem is going to kill people at a private event? Kline might believe you, but he'd need a warrant, and no judge in the country is going to issue one based on the theory that iambic pentameter is a lethal weapon."

She was right. The investigation Kline had been building was solid, two deaths, circumstantial evidence linking them to a consistent mechanism, a growing case file that any competent prosecutor could use to open a formal inquiry. But formal inquiries took weeks. Warrants took probable cause that could be articulated in language a judge could understand. And what Lena had, the knowledge that specific rhythmic patterns could hijack the human nervous system, was not the kind of probable cause that survived translation into legal terminology.

She needed Julian.

The realization arrived without surprise, because part of her had known it since Nadia's first sentence. Julian was the only person who understood the mechanism well enough to intervene, who could identify the practitioners' errors in real time, who could counteract an unstable delivery, who could walk into a room where the sonnet was being deployed and exercise the kind of precision that turned a weapon back into an instrument.

He was also the man whose voice lived in her nervous system like a second heartbeat, whose proximity made her breathing do things her mind hadn't authorized, and whose eyes, when they found hers, made the concept of resistance feel like something she'd invented to avoid admitting what she actually wanted.

Going to Julian meant going deeper. Not just into the investigation, not just into the Order, but into the specific, dangerous, intoxicating space between her analytical mind and her receptive body. It meant being near him. Hearing him. Feeling the gravitational pull of his attention and his voice and his particular, devastating way of making control look like kindness.

She called him anyway.

He picked up on the first ring, which meant he already knew.

"Victor," she said.

"Yes."

"Saturday."

"I'm aware."

"Can you stop it?"

A pause. Not his standard calibrated silence. Something more human. The pause of a man weighing not just options but costs.

"Not alone," he said.

"Then we work together."

"Yes." Another pause. "But I have a condition."

Lena's grip tightened on the phone. "I'm listening."

"One evening. Before Saturday. You and I, in a private setting, without the sonnet, without experimentation, without the architecture of professional distance that you have maintained, admirably, I should say, since we met."

"Julian—"

"No analysis. No documentation. No treating every word I say as evidence for a case file." His voice was quiet now, stripped of its usual placement and calibration, and what remained was something Lena had never heard from him: a voice that was asking rather than directing, requesting rather than arranging, vulnerable rather than precise.

"Just listen to me. Not the Instrument. Me. The man behind the mechanism. I think, given what we're about to attempt, that you deserve to know who that man actually is."

Lena stood in her kitchen, phone pressed to her ear, and felt the specific, terrible tension of a woman being offered something she wanted by someone she didn't fully trust, in circumstances that made the distinction between personal desire and professional obligation almost impossible to locate.

"This isn't a technique," she said.

"No."

"You're not deploying cadence manipulation or entrainment architecture or any of the tools you've spent your career perfecting."

"I am asking, Lena. Asking. Without structure, without rhythm, without anything except the hope, and it is hope, not certainty, that you will say yes."

She closed her eyes.

Behind them, the familiar landscape of her internal world: the analytical frameworks, the professional boundaries, the lessons of Marcus, the lessons of the sonnet, the carefully maintained distance between the woman who studied influence and the woman who was susceptible to it.

And underneath all of that, underneath the training and the caution and the twelve years of vigilance that had become so habitual it felt like personality, something else. Something that had been listening to Julian Calder since the first night in his acoustic room and had recognized, in the specific quality of his attention, something it had been looking for without knowing it.

Not the sonnet's recognition. Not the neurological pattern-matching of a receptive nervous system encountering its ideal stimulus.

Human recognition. The kind that happened between two people who saw each other clearly enough to be afraid of what they'd found and interested enough to keep looking.

"Tomorrow evening," she said. "Your place. No sonnet. No Instrument. No performance of any kind."

"Agreed."

"And Julian, if I suspect for even a moment that you're using technique, I walk out and we handle Saturday without the benefit of trust. Are we clear?"

"We are clear."

"Good."

She hung up. Set the phone on the counter. Looked at the window, where the morning light was doing its daily work of turning Manhattan's skyline from silhouette to substance.

Then she called Kline.

"I need you to trust me," she said.

"That's the worst possible way to start a phone call."

"I'm working with Julian to stop Victor's event on Saturday. It's the only way to prevent mass casualties."

Kline was quiet for three seconds. "And the part you're not telling me?"

"I'm meeting Julian tomorrow evening. Privately. To establish a working relationship."

"Establish a working relationship." The flatness in his voice could have leveled a building. "Is that what we're calling it?"

"Aaron."

"I'm not judging, Lena. I'm worrying. There's a difference. The man has spent twenty-three years learning how to make people do what he wants, and you're about to spend an evening alone with him in his living room."

"Without the sonnet. Without technique. Without any acoustic advantage."

"He doesn't need acoustic advantage. He has a face and a voice and a brain the size of a planet, and you—"

Kline stopped himself. Lena could hear the effort of the stop, the sound of a sentence being caught mid-fall and hauled back by its collar.

"And I what?" she asked quietly.

Kline sighed. "And you care about him. Which is the most dangerous thing in this whole goddamn situation, because the sonnet exploits what's already there, and what's already there, Lena, is not clinical interest."

The observation sat between them on the phone line like a stone in a stream, undeniable, immovable, and right in the middle of the path she'd chosen.

"I know," she said.

"You know."

"Yes."

"And you're going anyway."

"Yes."

Another sigh. Longer this time. The sigh of a man who had spent twenty years watching people make decisions he couldn't prevent and who had developed, over those years, a specific form of loyalty that expressed itself not as agreement but as proximity.

"I'll be parked outside," he said. "With my phone on. And a very short patience."

"Thank you."

"Don't thank me. Just come out of there breathing your own rhythm."

She almost smiled.

"I'll do my best," she said.

And meant it.

And knew, with the quiet honesty that the morning light demanded, that her best might not be enough.

• • •

CHAPTER NINETEEN: *The Preparation*

Julian opened the door himself.

No intermediary. No assistant. No careful staging of the entrance to establish control over the first impression. Just a man in a dark sweater with his sleeves pushed to his forearms, standing in the doorway of his private quarters with the unguarded expression of someone who had been waiting and was relieved that the waiting was over.

"You came," he said.

"I said I would."

"Yes. But saying and arriving are different commitments."

Lena stepped inside, and the room received her with the same warm, lived-in imperfection she'd encountered before, the piano, the leather chair, the books stacked in defiance of shelving conventions, the particular amber light that made the space feel like the interior of something carved from wood and memory. But it was different tonight. A fire was burning in a fireplace she hadn't noticed on her previous visit, and the light from it moved across the walls with the natural, ungovernable irregularity of flame.

No acoustic engineering in firelight. No precision in the way shadows moved. Just warmth doing what warmth did, reaching into corners and softening edges without being asked.

Julian closed the door. The click of the latch was quiet, domestic, unremarkable. A door being closed by a man in his own home.

"Wine?" he offered.

"Water."

He smiled, not at the refusal but at the precision of it. She wanted clarity. She wanted her perceptions unmediated by anything that might blur the line between what was real and what was wished for. He understood that. She could see the understanding in the way he nodded, poured water from a glass pitcher, and handed it to her without commentary.

They sat.

Same chairs as before. Same distance. But the quality of the space between them had changed, not because the room was different, but because they were. The last time they'd sat here, they had been adversaries negotiating the terms of an exchange. Tonight, they were something else. Not allies, exactly. Not lovers, certainly. Something that existed in the space between those categories, undefined and unnamed, operating by rules they were inventing as they went.

"No sonnet," Lena said.

"No sonnet."

"No technique."

"No technique."

"You're already using technique."

Julian blinked. "I'm sorry?"

"The fire. The sweater instead of the jacket. The rolled sleeves, exposing the forearms, which signals vulnerability and physical labor, both of which create unconscious associations with trustworthiness. You opened the door yourself. You offered wine but accepted water without resistance. Every detail of this evening has been arranged to make you appear unguarded."

Julian looked at her for a long moment. Then he laughed.

Not his controlled, calibrated, precisely placed laugh. A real one. Warm and surprised and slightly ruined by genuine amusement, the laugh of a man who had spent so long being in control that being caught was a pleasure he'd forgotten existed.

"You're right," he said. "About the sleeves. About the door. Not about the fire, I was cold." He leaned back in his chair, and the posture he assumed was either the most natural thing she'd ever seen him do or the most convincing performance, and the fact that she couldn't tell the difference was exactly the problem and exactly the point. "So. How do you want to do this?"

"Do what?"

"This evening. This conversation. The thing you came here for, which is not tactical planning for Saturday, we could have done that by phone, but something else. Something you don't have a professional framework for."

Lena held his gaze. "I want to know who you are. Not what you do. Not what you've built. Not the performer or the practitioner or the leader of a secret society. The person underneath all of that."

"That person may not be as interesting as the architecture suggests."

"I'll take that risk."

Julian studied her. The firelight moved across his face, and in the shifting light his features lost some of their habitual precision, the shadows softening the angles, the warmth loosening something in his expression that she'd never seen loosen before.

"I was a lonely child," he said.

The statement arrived without preamble, without setup, without the verbal architecture that usually preceded Julian's revelations. Just a fact. Delivered the way facts were delivered when they mattered too much to be dressed up.

"Not unloved," he continued. "My parents were kind. Attentive, even. But they were, ordinary. Their emotional bandwidth operated in a range that I exhausted before I turned ten. They could love me, but they couldn't *reach* me. Not because they didn't try. Because whatever was inside me that needed to be reached existed at a frequency they couldn't hear."

Lena said nothing. She let the silence hold, because silence was the space in which Julian Calder was least comfortable, and tonight, discomfort was a form of honesty.

"The piano helped," he said. "For a while. Music was a language that could carry more than words, more emotion, more complexity, more of the specific kind of longing that I didn't have vocabulary for. And when I played, people responded. Not to me, to the music. But through the music, to something in me that I couldn't express any other way."

"And that wasn't enough."

"It was never enough. Because the response was to the *performance*, not to the performer. The audience loved what I could do with a piano. They didn't know, and didn't need to know, who was doing it. I was a medium. A conduit. The most invisible kind of visible person."

He looked at the fire, and in the orange light his profile was the profile of a man who had spent his whole life being heard without being known.

"The Instrument changed that," he said. "Not immediately. Not simply. But the sonnet operates on a different level than music. Music reaches the emotions. The Instrument reaches the *nervous system*. When I speak the cadence and a listener responds, when their breathing follows mine, when their body begins to mirror the rhythm I'm offering, there is a connection that transcends performance. For those few minutes, I am not just heard. I am *felt*. By another human body. In a way that no other form of communication has ever achieved."

"And you can't feel it back," Lena said.

The words landed, and the fire crackled, and Julian Calder sat in his leather chair in his warm room with his rolled sleeves and his unguarded expression and absorbed the truth that defined him with the quiet stoicism of a man who had been living with it for a very long time.

"No," he said. "I cannot."

"You're Resistant."

"Permanently. Constitutionally. My neural architecture doesn't engage with the mechanism. I've been tested, by Nadia, by three independent neurologists, by the most sophisticated auditory processing assessments available. The entrainment simply doesn't occur. My brain processes the cadence as information, not as instruction. I hear the words. I understand the structure. I appreciate the beauty. But I do not *feel* it."

"And that's why you've spent twenty-three years perfecting it."

He looked at her then, and what was in his eyes was the most naked thing she'd ever seen from him, more naked than confession, more naked than vulnerability, more naked than the laugh that had surprised him a few minutes ago. It was the look of a man who had just had the central organizing principle of his life articulated by someone who wasn't him, and who was realizing, in real time, that being seen this clearly was both the thing he'd wanted most and the thing he'd feared most, and that the two had always been the same thing.

"Yes," he said.

"You're trying to build something beautiful enough to reach you."

"Yes."

"And it never does."

"No. It never does."

Silence. But not empty silence. The silence of a room where something important had been laid bare and both people in it were deciding what to do with the exposure.

Lena set her water glass on the table.

"My turn," she said.

Julian nodded.

"Marcus didn't just manipulate me," she said. "He made me love the manipulation. That's the part I don't talk about. Not in depositions, not in therapy, not in the professional language I use to describe what happened. I talk about the techniques, the cadence modulation, the embedded commands, the strategic use of silence and intimacy. I describe the mechanism. Because the mechanism is safe. The mechanism is clinical. The mechanism can be diagrammed on a whiteboard and taught in a seminar and stripped of everything that actually made it work."

She paused. The fire popped. The shadows moved.

"What actually made it work," she continued, "was that I wanted it. Not the control, the attention. The feeling of being the focus of someone's entire perceptual apparatus. Marcus didn't just manage our conversations, he *attended* to them. Every word I said was received, processed, responded to with a precision that made me feel like the most interesting person in any room. And that feeling, being studied, being known, being the object of someone's complete and unwavering focus, was the thing I was addicted to. Not the compliance. The attention."

She looked at Julian.

"You understand why I'm telling you this."

"Yes." His voice was quieter than she'd ever heard it. Not placed. Not calibrated. Quiet the way a room is quiet after something loud has stopped. "Because I give you the same thing. The attention. The focus. And you're afraid that what you feel for me is the same pattern repeating."

"Yes."

"Is it?"

The question sat between them like an object on a table, visible, tangible, requiring a response that would determine the shape of everything that followed.

Lena looked at Julian Calder. At the rolled sleeves and the firelight and the face that was, tonight, more human than she'd ever seen it. At the man who had built a cathedral of sound that he could never pray in, who had spent his life creating an experience of connection that he could offer to others but never receive, who was sitting across from her with the specific, devastating vulnerability of someone who had stopped performing and was left with only himself.

"No," she said. "It's not the same."

"How do you know?"

"Because Marcus made me feel known, and it was an illusion. You make me feel known, and it terrifies me. If it were the same pattern, it would feel safe. It doesn't. It feels like the most dangerous thing I've ever done."

The words hung in the firelit air, and neither of them moved.

Five feet between them. The same distance as every other time they'd sat in these chairs. The distance that had felt professional, then strategic, then tolerable, and now felt like the most unbridgeable gap she'd ever encountered. Five feet might as well have been five miles. Five feet might as well have been five inches. The distance meant nothing and everything, and the meaning shifted every time one of them breathed.

Julian leaned forward. Not far. An inch. Two.

"I want to tell you something," he said, "and I want you to hear it without analysis. Without looking for the mechanism underneath it. Just, hear it."

Lena's heart rate was elevated. She could feel it. "Go ahead."

"You are the most extraordinary person I have ever encountered. Not because you're brilliant, though you are. Not because you resist the Instrument, though that's remarkable. Because you make me want to be understood by someone, and I have spent my entire adult life believing that desire was a weakness I had successfully eliminated."

The words landed in Lena's chest with a warmth that was nothing like the sonnet. Not patterned. Not rhythmic. Not the precise, engineered pleasure of a neurological mechanism being expertly activated. Something messier. Something with rough edges and uncertain duration and no instruction manual. Something that felt less like being played and more like being reached.

She didn't lean forward.

She didn't need to.

"Julian," she said, and his name in her voice was its own act of intimacy, two syllables spoken without cadence, without technique, without anything except the genuine, unprotected desire of a woman saying the name of a man who mattered to her. "We have a warehouse full of people to save on Saturday."

"Yes."

"And after Saturday, everything changes. The Order, the investigation, the sonnet, all of it goes public."

"Yes."

"And when it does, you and I will be on different sides of a very complicated equation."

"Probably."

She held his gaze. "I need you to know, before any of that happens, that this is real. What I feel in this room right now. It's not the sonnet. It's not a pattern. It's not a mechanism I can diagram."

"I know."

"It's terrifying."

"I know that too."

They sat with it. The fire burned. The shadows moved. Two people who had spent their entire lives studying the distance between human beings acknowledged, in the particular grammar of silence and firelight and five feet of uncharged air, that the distance had been closed.

They did not touch.

They did not need to.

When Lena stood to leave, an hour later, or two, or ten minutes, she would never be quite sure, Julian walked her to the door with the unhurried courtesy of a man who understood that some departures were not endings but commas. Pauses in a sentence that was still being written.

At the door, she turned.

"Saturday," she said.

"Saturday," he confirmed.

She looked at him one last time. The man in the doorway. The fire behind him. The warm room where something important had happened without anyone raising their voice.

"Thank you," she said. "For not being perfect tonight."

Julian's lips curved in a smile that was, for once, entirely his own.

"I thought about it," he said. "But you would have noticed."

She laughed. A real laugh. The kind she hadn't made in longer than she wanted to calculate.

Then she walked into the cold November night, where Kline was parked at the curb with his engine running and his phone in his hand and the expression of a man who had been counting minutes.

She got in the car.

"Well?" Kline said.

"We're ready for Saturday."

"That's not what I asked."

Lena looked out the windshield at the city lights, at the imperfect, irregular, uncontrollable beauty of a world that refused to operate in iambic pentameter no matter how much you wanted it to.

"I know," she said.

And for the first time since this investigation began, her breathing was neither resisting nor surrendering.

It was just breathing.

• • •

CHAPTER TWENTY: *The Demonstration*

The warehouse had been dressed to kill, which turned out to be less metaphorical than anyone in attendance would have preferred.

Victor Hale had spent serious money on the transformation, the raw industrial space converted into something that split the difference between corporate gala and high-end nightclub. Lighting that suggested intimacy without requiring it. A bar that served the kind of cocktails that cost seventeen dollars and tasted like ambition. Tables arranged in a semicircle facing a raised platform at the far end, where a single microphone stood on a stand, unadorned, patient as a loaded gun.

Fifty guests. Lena counted them as she entered through the service entrance, Kline behind her, Julian and Nadia arriving separately through the main doors to avoid the appearance of a coordinated entry. The guest list Nadia had obtained proved accurate, the room was populated by the specific subset of the very wealthy who had learned that the next significant competitive advantage would not be technological or financial but *neurological*. People who had read the right white papers, attended the right conferences, and arrived tonight because Victor Hale had promised them a demonstration of something that would make every other persuasion technique in their arsenal obsolete.

They had dressed for disruption. Lena had dressed for the service entrance.

She positioned herself near the back of the room, behind a column, close enough to the exit for a quick departure and far enough from the platform that the acoustic impact would be slightly reduced. Kline stood beside her with the rigid posture of a man who was carrying a badge under his jacket and a warrant in his pocket, the warrant he'd obtained that afternoon from a judge who'd been persuaded not by the theory of weaponized poetry but by the more conventional evidence of two suspicious deaths, a pattern of unreported medical incidents at private events, and a detailed affidavit from Dr. Nadia Osei documenting experiments conducted on human subjects without institutional review or informed consent.

The warrant gave Kline authority to intervene if he observed evidence of assault. The question was whether what was about to happen in this room would look, to a reasonable observer, like assault.

Lena suspected it would look like a cocktail party until someone stopped breathing.

Julian had positioned himself near the front, seated at one of the tables, wearing the composed anonymity of a man who could have been any well-dressed guest at any private event. But Lena could see the tension in his posture, a rigidity that contradicted his usual fluid control, the physical signature of a man watching someone else handle his life's work with inadequate care and insufficient respect.

Victor took the stage at eight-fifteen.

He was good at this, the public-facing portion, the pitch, the warm-up act. His voice carried the room with the practiced authority of a man who had spent forty years making people comfortable with giving him their money. He spoke about innovation. About the next frontier of human potential. About the ancient connection between language and the body that modern science was only beginning to understand.

He did not mention the Cadence Society. He did not mention Shakespeare. He did not mention the two people who had died.

"Tonight," Victor said, "you'll experience something that no amount of description can prepare you for. Not a presentation. Not a pitch. A demonstration. Of what the human voice can do when it operates at its full potential."

He stepped aside, and the performer took the stage.

She was not Margaux.

Margaux had refused, had called Lena the night before and told her so, her voice carrying the shaky resolve of a woman who had finally found a boundary and was holding it with both hands. The woman who took the microphone was someone Lena didn't recognize: mid-thirties, poised, with the trained posture of a professional vocalist. One of Victor's independent hires. Skilled enough to deliver the material. Not skilled enough to understand what she was delivering.

That was the danger.

A pilot who didn't know the plane was loaded with explosives. A surgeon who didn't know the patient was allergic to the anesthetic. A performer who had been given the cadence and the text and the rhythmic framework and had practiced until her delivery was smooth and confident, without ever being told that the mechanism she was activating could stop a human heart.

She began.

Not with the sonnet. With the preparatory material, the warm-up sequence that Margaux used at salons to prime the audience's nervous systems for the main event. Standard approach. Build the entrainment gradually. Let the room's collective breathing synchronize before introducing the more powerful cadence.

The room responded. Lena watched it happen from behind her column: the progressive, cascading surrender of fifty nervous systems to a single vocal rhythm. Shoulders dropping. Breathing deepening. Faces softening from the guarded alertness of sophisticated people at an event they hadn't quite figured out into the open, receptive expression of listeners whose bodies had begun operating under someone else's instructions.

It was rougher than Margaux's delivery. Less precise. The timing was slightly off, not enough to break the effect, but enough to introduce variability. Some listeners were tracking perfectly, their breathing locked in tight synchronization with the performer's cadence. Others were drifting, their neurological responses inconsistent, their bodies receiving contradictory signals from a delivery that wavered between precision and approximation.

Julian shifted in his seat. Lena saw it, the almost imperceptible tension that rippled through his frame, the response of a master craftsman watching an apprentice handle his tools with insufficient care.

The performer transitioned into the sonnet.

"When breath is lent to shape the yielding ear..."

Lena felt it. Even at this distance, even behind a column, even with her breathing deliberately irregular and her posture deliberately asymmetric, she felt the pattern reach for her. Degraded by distance and imprecision, softened by the acoustic imperfections of a warehouse that had been designed for product launches rather than neurological intervention, but present. Like hearing a familiar song played on an out-of-tune piano: wrong enough to notice, right enough to affect.

She held. Easily, this time. The delivery wasn't precise enough to threaten her defenses.

But others in the room were not so fortunate.

"And cadence binds what reason would defy..."

A woman at the third table exhaled audibly, a long, shuddering breath that drew glances from her neighbors. Her eyes had unfocused, her posture collapsed into the boneless yielding that Lena recognized from the salon, from Julian's demonstration, from every clinical case study she'd ever reviewed on extreme parasympathetic activation. She was gone. Deep. Unreachable without intervention.

Next to her, a man in his sixties gripped the edge of the table with both hands, his face contorted in an expression that was not pleasure but its opposite, distress, confusion, the panicked incomprehension of a body receiving signals it couldn't process. His breathing was fast, shallow, arrhythmic. Sympathetic overload. The same response that had dropped the man at Victor's Gramercy event.

The performer continued, oblivious to the differential response. She didn't have the training to read the room's physiology. She saw faces, some relaxed, some tense, and interpreted the variation as normal audience diversity. She pushed forward, deeper into the quatrain, increasing her vocal pressure to compensate for the listeners who weren't tracking, which had the effect of intensifying the impact on the listeners who were.

"The pulse forgets the boundary of fear..."

The man at the third table made a sound. Low, strained, involuntary, the sound of a diaphragm trying to breathe in two rhythms at once and failing at both. His skin had gone grey. His hands were shaking.

Kline saw it. "Lena—"

"I see him."

"We need to move."

"Not yet. If we interrupt now, the listeners who are deep in the effect will crash out, parasympathetic rebound. It could trigger cardiac events in anyone with a preexisting condition."

"And if we don't interrupt, that guy is going to code."

Lena looked at the man. At the performer. At the room full of people who were scattered across the full spectrum of the sonnet's effects, some surrendering, some suffering, some sitting in confused suspension between the two. A room that had been marketed as a demonstration and was rapidly becoming a disaster.

"Let me get to the stage," she said.

"What are you going to do?"

"What I've been building toward since this investigation started."

Kline didn't argue. Instead, he did something that surprised her, something that had nothing to do with poetry or neuroscience or the elegant architecture of linguistic control, and everything to do with twenty years of police work in rooms where things were about to go badly.

He moved first.

Not toward the stage. Toward the grey-faced man at the third table. Kline crossed the distance in four strides, badge already in his hand, and positioned himself beside the man with the calm, practiced authority of someone who had stabilized situations in alleys and emergency rooms and domestic disputes where the stakes were measured in blood rather than rhythm. He caught the paramedic's eye through the service entrance, the paramedic he'd stationed there an hour ago, over Lena's objection that it would draw attention, and gestured: *now*.

The paramedic moved in. Kline guided the grey-faced man to the floor, clearing the table, creating space, drawing the attention of the nearest guests away from the stage and toward something they understood, a medical emergency, a person in distress, the concrete and familiar language of someone needing help.

It was tactical. It was precise. And it created exactly what Lena needed: a gap. A moment when the room's attention fragmented, when the collective entrainment that the performer had been building stuttered as thirty heads turned toward the commotion at table three.

In that moment of broken focus, Lena moved toward the stage.

Julian, still seated, watched the performer with an expression that Lena had never seen on his face. It was the look of a man watching someone play a Stradivarius with a hammer, not anger, not contempt, but a grief so specific and so total that it had passed through all the usual emotional registers and arrived at something beyond them. He had spent twenty-three years perfecting this instrument, and someone was using it to hurt people, and the sound of his life's work being reduced to a blunt object was written across his features in a language more honest than anything he had ever spoken.

She moved.

• • •

CHAPTER TWENTY-ONE: *The Interruption*

Lena moved through the room the way she'd moved through crime scenes for twelve years, quickly, precisely, without unnecessary motion or wasted attention. The guests barely registered her passage. Most of them were too deep in the sonnet's effect to notice anything that wasn't part of the pattern they were following, and the ones who weren't deep enough were too confused by what they were feeling to care about a woman walking toward the stage with the focused intensity of someone who had just decided to become the most important person in the room.

The performer was mid-line when Lena reached the platform. "...and learns at last the sweetness of comply—"

Lena stepped onto the stage.

The performer faltered. Her cadence broke, a hiccup in the delivery, a fraction of a second of silence where the rhythm said there should be sound. Across the room, dozens of nervous systems that had been synchronized to her voice registered the break as a missed heartbeat: a jolt, a stutter, a momentary confusion that rippled through the audience like a wave hitting a seawall.

"What are you—" the performer started.

Lena took the microphone from her hand with the clean, unhesitating authority of a surgeon taking a scalpel from a nurse who was about to cut in the wrong place.

Then she spoke.

Not the sonnet. Not a speech. Not any form of structured address that the audience might have expected or that the room's acoustics might have supported.

She spoke the counter-cadence.

She'd built it over three weeks, not from theory, not from Julian's archives, not from the elegant architecture of the sonnet itself. From its opposite. From every principle she'd identified in the sonnet's construction, inverted. Where the sonnet used regular intervals, the counter-cadence used irregular ones. Where the sonnet built anticipation through predictable timing, the counter-cadence destroyed anticipation through deliberate unpredictability. Where the sonnet's phonetic structure encouraged the listener's breathing to synchronize, the counter-cadence's phonetic structure made synchronization impossible.

It was ugly. That was intentional. Beauty was a trap, the same trap the sonnet used, the same trap that made listeners lean in and open up and lower their defenses. Ugly was safety. Ugly was the auditory equivalent of cold water on the face, a slap on the back of a choking man, a fire alarm in a building full of people who had forgotten there was a door.

"Break," she said into the microphone, and the word was spoken at a frequency and timing that contradicted the room's established rhythm. "Break the, pattern. Listen, not to, the, rhythm. Listen to, this."

The audience recoiled. Not physically, neurologically. The listeners who had been deep in the sonnet's effect surfaced with the gasping, disoriented emergence of people being pulled from deep water. Their faces shifted from the serene openness of compliance to the pinched, uncomfortable expression of a pleasure being taken away. Some of them looked angry. Some looked ill. One woman pressed her hands over her ears, as though the counter-cadence was causing physical pain, which, in a neurological sense, it was. Her nervous system had been promised completion and was receiving instead a deliberate, systematic denial of everything the pattern had been building toward.

The man at the third table stopped shaking. His breathing, which had been racing toward a crisis, stuttered and then reset, not into calm, but into the natural, messy, uncontrolled irregularity of a body that was no longer being operated by an external rhythm. He slumped in his chair, grey-faced but conscious, his hands still gripping the table edge.

Victor Hale's security moved first.

Two men, large, professional, converging on the stage from opposite sides of the room with the coordinated efficiency of people who had rehearsed this exact scenario. They weren't violent, Victor was too smart for overt violence at an event full of witnesses, but their trajectory and their posture communicated an intention to remove Lena from the stage as quickly and cleanly as possible.

The first one reached the platform.

"Ma'am, you need to—"

Julian's voice cut through the room.

He didn't shout. He didn't raise his volume above conversational. He simply *spoke*, from his seat, six rows back, in the natural register of his trained, devastating voice, and the words he chose and the cadence he used to deliver them were not the sonnet, were not the counter-cadence, were not anything Lena had ever heard him deploy before.

They were a command. Spoken in the specific rhythmic structure that, Lena realized with a chill, was the mechanism's simplest application: a single instruction, cadence-locked to the listener's respiratory cycle, delivered with the precision of a man who had spent twenty-three years learning exactly how to make a human body hesitate.

The security guard stopped.

Not permanently. Not dramatically. He hesitated. His forward momentum arrested for two seconds, an eternity in the context of physical confrontation, as his nervous system processed the competing signals of his employer's instructions and the authority embedded in Julian's voice. His body didn't know which to follow. His mind, trained for obedience to command structures, recognized in Julian's cadence something that registered as higher authority than the earpiece telling him to move.

Two seconds was enough.

Kline was already there.

He materialized beside the security guard with the warrant in one hand and his badge in the other, and the words he spoke, the specific, practiced, legally precise words of a detective executing a court order, had no cadence, no rhythm, no embedded commands. They had something better. They had the weight of the State of New York behind them.

"NYPD. I have a warrant. Everyone in this room stays put."

Victor Hale stood.

For a moment, the entire room was frozen in a configuration that looked, to Lena's eyes, like a diorama of the investigation itself: the performer standing stage left with the stunned expression of a woman who'd just learned she'd been firing a weapon she'd thought was a toy. The security guards held in place by the competing authorities of their employer and a detective with paper. The audience, fifty people in various stages of neurological recovery, some angry, some dazed, some weeping, one being attended by the paramedic Kline had stationed outside. Nadia, who had entered through a side door with a laptop open and recording software active, capturing everything.

And Julian, still seated, still composed, looking at Victor with an expression that Lena had seen once before, in the vault, when Nadia had confronted him, but that had now crystallized into something harder, more final.

Victor's voice carried the room because he had the lungs for it and the practiced projection of a man who'd spent four decades making himself heard. "This is a private event. You have no jurisdiction here."

Kline held up the warrant. "This document says otherwise. And the paramedic treating your guest over there is going to have a medical report that says a lot more."

Victor's gaze found Julian across the room. "You did this."

Julian stood. Slowly, with the unhurried precision that defined everything he did, and crossed the distance between his table and the stage with the measured steps of a man who had arrived at a destination he'd been walking toward for a very long time.

"I didn't do anything, Victor. That's the point." He stopped at the edge of the platform, close enough that his voice needed no amplification. "I told you the Instrument requires precision. I told you it cannot be scaled. I told you that imprecise delivery in an uncontrolled environment with untrained practitioners and unscreened listeners would cause exactly what it caused tonight." He looked at the grey-faced man being treated by the paramedic. "You chose not to listen."

"I chose to evolve the program beyond your limitations—"

"You chose to sell something that isn't yours."

The room went quiet with the particular, charged quiet that preceded either resolution or disaster.

Victor looked at Julian. At Kline. At Lena on the stage. At Nadia with her recording laptop. At the fifty witnesses who had just experienced, in their own nervous systems, the precise and terrifying power of the thing he'd been trying to package.

He was a practical man. A calculating man. A man who understood leverage and its limits.

"My lawyers will be in touch," he said.

He walked out.

His security followed.

The room exhaled.

Not collectively, not the synchronized, sonnet-driven exhalation that had characterized the earlier part of the evening. Individually. Messily. Fifty people breathing on their own schedules, in their own rhythms, at their own pace.

It was the most beautiful sound Lena had ever heard.

• • •

CHAPTER TWENTY-TWO: *The Fallout*

The world didn't end. It just tilted, slightly, permanently, and kept going.

The investigation moved from Kline's desk to the district attorney's office in the first week, propelled by the medical report from Saturday's event, one cardiac incident, three cases of acute anxiety requiring treatment, and the testimony of a paramedic who'd seen enough unusual presentations to know when something didn't fit the normal clinical categories. The DA's office, confronted with Nadia's research data, Lena's expert analysis, and the physical evidence of two unexplained deaths, opened a formal inquiry into the Cadence Society under statutes governing unauthorized human experimentation and reckless endangerment.

Victor Hale's lawyers arrived exactly when he'd promised they would, armed with NDAs and legal theories and the particular brand of aggressive civility that men with very expensive representation deployed when they knew the evidence was bad but believed the process could be worse. The lawyers met the DA's team. The DA's team met the lawyers. Motions were filed. Counter-motions were filed. The machinery of legal accountability engaged its gears with the slow, grinding, implacable momentum of a system that had been designed to be thorough rather than fast.

Victor was not arrested. Not yet. But the investigation had frozen his parallel research program, seized his practitioners' notes and training materials, and placed the warehouse venue under judicial seal. His access to the Order's resources was severed by Julian's directive, and the funding streams that had sustained the Order's operations for over a decade dried up overnight, leaving the infrastructure intact but unpowered, like a ship with its engine cut and its sails furled.

The Order itself fractured along the lines that had been forming since Lena's first visit. Julian disbanded the formal structure, cancelled the salons, dismissed the performers, closed the archive rooms, with the cold, surgical efficiency of a man dismantling something he'd built before someone else could demolish it. A controlled demolition. Every piece documented, catalogued, and preserved before being removed from circulation.

Margaux disappeared.

Lena tried calling her three times in the first week. Each call went to voicemail, and each voicemail was the same: Margaux's voice, warm and professional and recorded in a time before everything had changed, saying she'd call back as soon as she could. She never did. Lena texted once, *No pressure. Just want to know you're safe*, and received a single reply two days later: a period. Nothing else. The smallest possible acknowledgment that she still existed and the clearest possible statement that she wanted to exist somewhere the sonnet couldn't reach her.

Lena understood. She stopped calling.

Harris Cole was admitted to a private neurological facility in Connecticut, one that Nadia recommended, staffed by researchers who specialized in obsessive-compulsive disorders and pattern-fixation syndromes. His treatment was experimental: a combination of cognitive behavioral therapy, rhythmic desensitization, and the structural disruption protocol that Lena had been developing since mid-investigation. It was not a cure. There was no cure. But it was management, the careful, incremental work of teaching a nervous system to tolerate the gap between the pattern it craved and the resolution it would never receive.

Lena visited him on his third day. He was thinner, paler, but present in a way he hadn't been during their last meeting. The restless energy was still there, the seeking, the scanning, the involuntary attention to any rhythmic stimulus in his environment, but it was softer now, held in check by a combination of medication, therapy, and the simple, enormous relief of being in a place where people understood what was wrong with him.

"Is it always going to be there?" he asked her.

"I don't know," she said. And for the first time, honesty felt like the kindest thing she could offer.

"That's not a great answer."

"No. It isn't."

He smiled. Small, tired, genuine. "At least it's real."

Daniel Mercer remained unchanged. His lips still moved. His eyes still stared. On the cold December morning when Lena visited him, a nurse mentioned that his family had stopped coming. Not out of cruelty, out of the particular, grinding exhaustion of loving someone who was present in body and absent in every way that presence was supposed to mean. Lena stood beside his bed and didn't try to reach him. She just watched his breathing, perfect, regulated, permanently synchronized with a rhythm that would never let him go, and let herself feel the weight of what perfection cost.

The testimony was harder than she'd expected.

She'd prepared for weeks, organized her findings, structured her explanations, rehearsed the language she would use to describe a phenomenon that existed at the intersection of neuroscience, linguistics, and human vulnerability. She had expected skepticism. She had expected the polite, careful questioning of attorneys who needed to understand a mechanism they'd never encountered. What she hadn't expected was the courtroom itself, the particular acoustics of a wood-paneled room with high ceilings and hard surfaces, the way sound traveled and reflected and lingered, the way fifty people breathing in a confined space created a collective rhythm that pressed against her awareness with a familiarity she couldn't suppress.

She delivered her testimony in deliberately irregular cadence. Pausing at unexpected intervals. Varying her volume. Breaking her own rhythm every thirty seconds, the way she'd learned to break the sonnet's. The attorneys noticed, one of them asked if she was feeling well, if she needed water, if the questioning was proceeding too quickly. She told them she was fine. She did not tell them that the reason she was speaking in broken, unpredictable patterns was that speaking fluently, in a room designed for the human voice, with fifty people listening, had begun to feel dangerously close to performing.

Julian dismantled the Order in the same week Lena gave her testimony. She heard about it from Nadia, who described the process in the clipped, grief-edged tones of a scientist watching a laboratory being decommissioned. The archive rooms emptied. The acoustic chamber sealed. The salon space in Westchester shuttered, its owner, a trust fund managed by a family that had been part of the Order since the eighteenth century, withdrawing access without explanation or complaint, the way people withdrew from things they'd always known were borrowed.

Julian supervised it personally. Every box catalogued. Every recording labeled. Every fragment of the sonnet's history preserved with the same meticulous care he'd given to its refinement, as though the act of dismantling could be its own form of devotion if you did it with enough precision.

Nadia said he didn't speak during most of it. Just worked. Packed boxes. Sealed rooms. Locked doors that had been open for decades. When the last archive room was empty, the sub-basement vault where she had confronted him, where three centuries of accumulated research had been stored in climate-controlled silence, he stood in the doorway for several minutes, looking at the bare shelves, before turning off the light and closing the door behind him.

Lena drove back from the Connecticut facility through December landscape that was all grey sky and bare trees, and she thought about the distance between the people the sonnet had touched. Harris, who might recover. Daniel, who wouldn't. Margaux, who was trying. Julian, who had spent his life building something he'd now dismantled with his own hands. And herself, carrying the sonnet's imprint in her nervous system the way a river carried the shape of the rocks it had flowed over.

Changed. Not destroyed.

But changed.

The investigation was over.

What came next was harder.

What came next was choice.

• • •

CHAPTER TWENTY-THREE: *The Choice*

He came on a Sunday.

Late. Not the strategic lateness of a man managing his entrance, but the genuine lateness of someone who had been deciding whether to come at all and had spent the evening walking the length of the decision before arriving at its end. It was almost eleven when the buzzer sounded, and Lena, who had not been sleeping, who had been sitting in the dark of her apartment with a glass of water and the quiet company of her own breathing, crossed to the intercom and pressed the button without asking who it was.

She already knew.

Julian stood in the hallway looking less like himself than she'd ever seen him. Not diminished, he would never be diminished, not even if you stripped him of every technique and every resource and left him standing in an empty room with nothing but his natural voice. But reduced to something essential. A man in a dark coat with tired eyes and no agenda, who had come to her apartment on a Sunday night because there was nowhere else left to go where someone might understand what he had lost.

"May I come in?" he asked.

She stepped aside.

Her apartment received him the way it received everything, with the neutral, undecorated efficiency of a space that had been designed to support function rather than feeling. He moved through the small living room with the careful courtesy of a guest who understood that the absence of personal objects was itself personal, that the blank walls and minimal furniture were not a failure of decoration but a statement of intent by a woman who had learned to distrust the comfort of familiar things.

He sat in the single armchair. She sat on the couch, three feet away.

For a while, neither of them spoke. The city hummed outside. A siren passed, its Doppler curve rising and falling like the opening phrase of something that chose not to continue. The radiator clicked. The apartment breathed with the autonomous, unregulated rhythm of a space that belonged to no one but the woman who lived in it.

"The DA's office offered me immunity," Julian said. "In exchange for full testimony about the Order's operations, its history, and the mechanism of the Instrument."

"Will you take it?"

"I already have." He looked at his hands, the pianist's hands that had found a different instrument and had spent twenty-three years learning to play it. "The records are being transferred. The archive will become part of the case file. Three centuries of research, refinement, obsession, all of it entered into evidence and sealed behind the particular kind of bureaucratic silence that ensures nothing dangerous will be examined carefully by anyone qualified to understand it."

Lena heard the bitterness in his voice. Not about the legal outcome, Julian was too pragmatic for that. About the waste. The reduction of a life's work to a case number. The transformation of the most remarkable acoustic phenomenon in human history into Exhibit A in a prosecution that would, ultimately, result in fines and probation and the kind of institutional hand-slapping that the legal system administered to white-collar transgressions it didn't have the vocabulary to properly punish.

"What will you do?" she asked.

"I don't know." The words came out with a simplicity that would have shocked anyone who'd only known the composed, deliberate, architecturally precise Julian Calder of the Cadence Society. "For the first time in twenty-three years, I don't have an answer to that question."

"That sounds terrifying."

"It is." He paused. "It's also the first time in twenty-three years that I've been honest about anything."

Lena studied him in the low light. The Julian who sat in her living room was not the man she'd met in the acoustic chamber, who had deployed silence like a weapon and spoken with the calibrated precision of an instrument he'd spent his life becoming. This was the person underneath, the lonely child who had watched a woman cry during a piano recital and had spent the rest of his life trying to understand the space between the music and the tears.

"You came here to ask me something," she said.

Julian met her eyes. "You have the most complete version of the sonnet in existence. More complete than what I gave the DA's office. More complete than what's in the archive."

"Yes."

"What are you going to do with it?"

The question filled the room the way sunlight fills a room, gradually, completely, leaving nothing untouched. It was the question that had been sitting in the back of Lena's mind since the night in her office when she'd read twelve lines aloud and stopped two short of the end. The question that had followed her through the investigation, through the salon, through the warehouse, through every encounter with the sonnet's rhythm and every encounter with the man who had devoted his life to perfecting it.

What do you do with something this beautiful, this dangerous, this fundamentally revelatory about the nature of human vulnerability?

"I could destroy it," she said.

"You could."

"I could publish it. Include the full text in my paper and let the academic community debate its significance and its risks."

"You could do that too."

"I could seal it. Lock it away. Join the long tradition of custodians who decided that the world wasn't ready and buried the evidence of its own potential."

"Yes."

Lena looked at him. At his tired eyes, his unguarded face, his hands resting in his lap with the looseness of a man who had finally stopped holding anything.

"Or I could hear it," she said.

The room went still.

Not the engineered stillness of Julian's performance space. Not the controlled stillness of a moment being managed. The natural, fragile, absolutely human stillness of two people arriving at the thing they'd been circling since they met.

"Lena," Julian said, and her name in his voice was stripped of everything he'd ever used it for, no cadence, no placement, no technique. Just the sound a man made when he said the name of someone who mattered to him and wanted her to know it. "If I read you the full sonnet, if you hear the complete text, delivered by someone who understands the mechanism, with your neurological profile—"

"I know what will happen."

"You're Receptive. Profoundly Receptive. The effect will be—"

"I know what it will be."

He stopped. Looked at her with something she'd never seen from him before. Not fascination. Not admiration. Not the particular quality of attention he'd directed at her since their first meeting.

Fear.

"I don't want to hurt you," he said.

"You won't."

"You can't know that."

"No. I can't." She leaned forward. "But I can choose. That's the difference, Julian. That's the difference between everything the Order did and what I'm asking you to do right now. Marcus didn't give me a choice. The sonnet, when it creeps into fragments on forums and catches people unaware, doesn't give them a choice. The salon didn't give people a real choice, they were primed, conditioned, swimming in a collective entrainment that made refusal feel like deprivation."

She held his gaze.

"I am sitting in my own apartment, in full possession of my faculties, with complete knowledge of the mechanism, the risks, the neurological cascade, the potential for dependency, and the precedent of Daniel Mercer. I am the most informed person on the planet about what this sonnet does to the human nervous system. And I am asking you, freely, deliberately, with no acoustic advantage, no entrainment priming, and no external pressure, to read it to me."

Julian's breathing changed. She watched it, the woman who had spent the entire investigation tracking breathing patterns, mapping respiratory shifts, reading the body's involuntary language the way other people read facial expressions. His breath deepened. Slowed. Not into the controlled, calibrated rhythm of a practitioner preparing to deliver. Into the deeper, less controlled rhythm of a man encountering an emotion he didn't have a technique for.

"Why?" he asked.

Lena smiled. It was not a strategic smile. Not a reassuring smile. Not the carefully composed expression of a woman managing a situation. It was the genuine, slightly scared, entirely real smile of a human being about to do something that terrified her, and choosing to do it anyway.

"Because I have spent the last three months fighting this thing," she said. "Resisting it. Breaking it. Disrupting it. Analyzing it until the analysis became its own form of avoidance. And I'm tired, Julian. Not of the fighting. Of the pretending. Of telling myself that my resistance is strength when we both know that what makes me resist isn't discipline, it's fear."

She paused. The apartment breathed around them.

"Marcus taught me to be afraid of surrender. The sonnet taught me to be afraid of my own desire. You—" She stopped. Started again. "You taught me that the difference between manipulation and intimacy isn't the mechanism. It's the choice. And I am choosing."

"Not because you have to hear it."

"Because I choose to."

Julian sat very still for a long time. The kind of stillness that wasn't composed or performed but simply *present*, a man sitting with a decision that would determine the shape of everything that followed and understanding, with the deep, aching clarity that only comes from decades of expertise, exactly what that shape would look like.

Then he reached into his coat and withdrew a single sheet of paper.

Lena recognized it. Her reconstruction. The twelve lines she'd assembled from fragments, marginalia, recordings, and the silent lips of a man who would never stop speaking them. But Julian's version had two additional lines at the bottom, the couplet. The final two lines that she'd stopped herself from speaking on the night she'd listened alone in her office. The resolution she'd denied herself at a cost that had left her sitting in the dark with her heart pounding and her body aching for something her mind had refused to allow.

"Are you sure?" he asked.

"Read it."

Julian looked at the page. Then at her. Then at the page again.

He took a breath. Not calibrated. Not prepared. A human breath, full of uncertainty and care and the specific kind of courage that was required to do something you'd been given the power to do and had always been afraid of doing.

And read.

"When breath is lent to shape the yielding ear..."

His voice filled her apartment the way water filled a vessel, finding every corner, every surface, every space that was available to receive it. Not the engineered resonance of the acoustic chamber. Not the amplified precision of the warehouse stage. The natural, unmediated, heartbreakingly beautiful sound of a human voice speaking words it had spent a lifetime learning, in a room that offered no enhancement and no protection.

Lena closed her eyes.

"And cadence binds what reason would defy..."

Her breathing aligned. She let it. No correction. No disruption. No sharp inhale to break the pattern. For the first time, she let the cadence take her breathing and reshape it, let her diaphragm expand and contract at the sonnet's pace, let her body accept the rhythm it had been craving since the evidence lab.

The warmth came immediately. Not gradually, not tentatively, immediately, fully, the way a dam broke when the last structural member failed. Three months of partial exposure had primed her nervous system to a sensitivity that no first-time listener could match. She was not hearing the sonnet for the first time. She was hearing it for the hundredth time, and every previous encounter, every fragment, every echo, every interrupted partial experience, fed into this moment with the accumulated force of a river that had been pooling behind a wall she had finally chosen to lower.

"The pulse forgets the boundary of fear, and learns at last the sweetness of comply..."

The first quatrain completed, and the resolution hit her with a force that was beyond anything she'd experienced before. Not pain. Not pleasure, exactly. Something larger than both, the profound, oceanic sensation of every cell in her body arriving at the same frequency at the same moment, the way an orchestra arrived at unison after a passage of counterpoint. Her muscles released. Her jaw opened. Her hands, which she'd been holding in loose fists on her thighs, opened, palms up, fingers relaxed, the universal gesture of reception.

She was aware. Fully aware. Her analytical mind continued to operate with perfect clarity, documenting the cascade, tracking the neurological progression, mapping the mechanism in real time. She could have stopped. She knew that. The window was still open. Her will was still present, still functional, still capable of the sharp, ugly disruption that had saved her every time before.

She chose not to use it.

"Let not the tongue declare what mind resists, for softer chains are forged in tempered sound..."

Julian's voice moved through the second quatrain with a care that Lena could feel, not the polished, effortless precision of his performances, but the careful, reverent, slightly trembling care of a man reading something sacred to the only person who had ever made him want to. He was not performing. He was *giving*. And the difference between the two was legible in every word, every pause, every breath he took between the lines.

"A silken tyranny through silence twists, till will lies still, yet pleasure is unbound..."

Tears. She hadn't expected them. They came without warning, without the usual precursors of emotional distress, no tightening of the throat, no burning behind the eyes. Just warmth, flowing down her cheeks with the same quiet inevitability that the sonnet's cadence flowed through her nervous system. She was crying not because she was sad, not because she was overwhelmed, but because her body was finally experiencing the thing it had been reaching for since the first carved line on a dead man's desk, and the experience was so precisely, so devastatingly, so perfectly what she had been missing that the only adequate response was the one her body chose without her.

"What art is this, that humbles crown and creed, and bends the spine without a hand or blade..."

Her spine curved. Not collapse. Yield. The specific, unmistakable, deeply intimate gesture of a body accepting that it did not need to hold itself upright, that the thing supporting it was not a chair or a posture or a defensive architecture but a rhythm, a voice, a trust.

"A whispered law no sovereign can impede, where flesh obeys, though thought would barricade..."

Twelve lines. The point where she'd stopped before. The edge of the cliff she'd walked to and turned back from on the night she'd listened alone in her office.

Beyond this line was the couplet. The resolution. The completion that every cell in her body had been screaming for since the moment she'd denied it.

Julian paused.

The pause was not calibrated. It was not strategic. It was the pause of a man looking at a woman whose face was wet with tears and whose body was more open than he had ever seen a human body be, and who was choosing, with the full, informed, uncoerced agency of someone who understood exactly what she was doing, to hear the end.

He read the couplet.

"So speak me slow, and let resistance part—"

Lena felt the words arrive at the place in her nervous system where they had always been meant to land, the place that the fragments had been pointing toward, that the partial exposures had been carving, that the three months of resistance and analysis and fear had been simultaneously defending and preparing. The penultimate line settled into her like the final piece of a puzzle that you hadn't realized was incomplete until the moment it became whole.

"For I am not thy voice... but now thy heart."

The sonnet completed.

And Lena Marchetti, forensic linguist, pattern analyst, student of the space between what was said and what was meant, woman who had spent twelve years learning to read the body's involuntary language and three months learning that her own body spoke the same language as everyone else's, Lena Marchetti let the pattern close around her like arms, like water, like the precise and terrifying and indescribably beautiful experience of being held by something that knew her better than she knew herself.

The silence that followed was not empty.

It was complete.

For a duration she would never be able to measure, seconds, minutes, something outside of time entirely, she existed in the space the sonnet had created: a space where resistance and surrender were not opposites but facets of the same experience, where the boundary between self and other dissolved not into loss but into expansion, where the fear she'd carried since Marcus, since the divorce, since the first moment she'd understood that wanting to be known was the same as wanting to be vulnerable, was not eliminated but *held*. Contained. Accepted. Integrated into a pattern that was large enough to include it without being defined by it.

She was not lost.

She was found.

When she opened her eyes, and the opening was gradual, gentle, the unhurried emergence of someone surfacing from a depth they'd needed to reach, Julian was sitting in the armchair with the page in his lap and tears on his own face.

He was looking at her.

Not with the analytical precision of a practitioner observing an effect. Not with the controlled fascination of a man watching his instrument perform its intended function. With the unguarded, unprotected, entirely human expression of a man who had just witnessed, for the first time in his life, the thing he had spent twenty-three years building, working exactly as he had always hoped it would, and who had experienced, through the medium of her response, the closest he would ever come to feeling it himself.

Lena's breathing was her own again. Irregular. Uncontrolled. Human.

She reached up and touched her face. Wet.

"How long?" she asked.

"About four minutes," Julian said. His voice was rough. Unplaced. Unperfect.

She nodded.

Sat with it.

Then said: "I'm not dependent."

Julian looked at her. "I know."

"The craving isn't there. The loop isn't there." She paused, checking, genuinely, honestly checking, with the diagnostic precision of a woman examining her own neurology for damage. "The pattern completed. And then it let go."

Julian's expression shifted. Something that had been held in tension for a very long time released across his features, not composure but its opposite, the slow, uncertain, deeply unfamiliar experience of relief.

"You're the first," he said.

"The first what?"

"The first person who heard the full sonnet, experienced the full effect, and came back."

Lena looked at him. At the page in his lap. At the words that had just done to her nervous system what three months of investigation had told her they would do, and that she had chosen to allow, and that had given her back to herself more completely than any act of resistance ever had.

"I came back," she said, "because I chose to go."

She leaned forward and took the page from his lap. Their fingers touched. A small contact. Not cadence. Not technique.

Just warmth.

"I'm going to need this," she said.

"For the paper?"

"For something else."

Julian looked at her, curious. "What?"

Lena held the page and looked at the final couplet, the two lines that had just completed a pattern four hundred years in the making, and thought about Harris, about Daniel, about Margaux, about every person who had encountered this sonnet and been captured by its perfection.

"A revision," she said.

• • •

CHAPTER TWENTY-FOUR: *The Altered Verse*

Six months later, in an office that now contained a photograph, a single image, taken by Kline at a precinct holiday party, of Lena laughing at something someone had said off-camera, Dr. Lena Marchetti finished her paper.

It was titled "Cadence, Compliance, and the Architecture of Auditory Influence." Forty-seven pages. The paper described the mechanism in detail, enough for any qualified researcher to understand how rhythmic entrainment could be deployed through the human voice to influence a listener's physiology and behavior. It explained the neuroscience. It documented the case studies. It presented the listener classification system.

What the paper did not contain was the sonnet.

Not a single line. Not a fragment. Not a variant. The paper described the phenomenon without providing the tool, the way a paper on nuclear physics might describe fission without providing the enrichment specifications. Enough to understand. Not enough to replicate.

It was, Lena knew, an imperfect solution. The information was out there, fragments on forums, corrupted variants in literary circles, the living echo in Daniel Mercer's silent, ceaselessly moving lips. Someone with sufficient determination and expertise could, eventually, reconstruct the mechanism from the theoretical framework her paper provided. Knowledge, once published, could not be un-published. The genie, as the saying went, was out of the bottle.

But the bottle could be redesigned.

That was what the revision was for.

She'd spent three months on it. Not the paper, the sonnet. Working alone, in her office, with the metronome running and a rule she'd established and maintained with the discipline of someone who understood, now, the difference between resistance and choice: she would not read the revised version aloud until it was finished. Not until every line had been tested on paper, analyzed for rhythmic profile, checked against the mechanism she'd spent a year learning to decode.

The revision kept the structure. The meter. The iambic pentameter that was the sonnet's skeleton, the rhythmic framework that gave the cadence its power. It kept the phonetic profile, the specific arrangement of vowels and consonants that shaped the listener's breathing through the physics of articulation.

But it changed the direction.

The original sonnet was a closed system. Each line built toward the couplet, and the couplet sealed the pattern, *For I am not thy voice... but now thy heart*, with the finality of a door closing, a circle completing, a mind arriving at a destination from which there was no return. The original sonnet captured. That was its function. That was its danger. It offered the listener perfection, and perfection, once experienced, became the only thing worth seeking.

Lena's revision opened what the original had closed.

She rewrote the couplet. Not to destroy the cadence, that would have been as futile as trying to unbuild a staircase by removing the top step. The mechanism was the mechanism. The rhythm worked because the brain was built to respond to it. You couldn't change human neurology. You could only change what the neurology was asked to do.

Her couplet did not resolve. It continued. It took the escalating, building, approaching-completion trajectory of the sonnet's twelve lines and, at the moment of expected resolution, turned the pattern outward instead of inward. Opened instead of closed. Suggested instead of concluded.

It left the listener *moving*, released into the ongoing, imperfect, unpredictable flow of a life that didn't end when the last line was spoken.

She'd tested it. Once. On herself. In her office, with the metronome off and the door locked and the photograph of herself laughing on the wall.

She'd read the full revised sonnet aloud and felt the cadence build, the same warmth, the same resonance, the same exquisite alignment of every cell in her body with the rhythm of the words. The twelve original lines had done what they always did: opened her up, softened her down, carried her toward the place where resistance and surrender met and discovered they were the same thing.

And then the revised couplet had arrived, and instead of closing around her, it had let her go. Released her the way a wave released you after carrying you to shore, the way music released you after the final chord, into a world that had been changed by what you'd heard, where the music still existed as a possibility but no longer as a requirement.

She'd sat in her office afterward, breathing normally, feeling the warmth fade not with the punishing, hollow withdrawal of incomplete exposure but with the gentle, natural dissipation of something that had come and gone and left her, impossibly, more herself than she'd been before.

No craving. No loop. No dependency.

Just the quiet, persistent, beautiful memory of what it felt like to be held by something perfect, and the knowledge that she could walk away.

• • •

Julian arrived at her office on a Thursday afternoon in May.

He looked different. Not in any way that most people would have noticed, the same tailored composure, the same careful posture, the same dark eyes that saw everything and revealed only what they chose. But Lena noticed. The angles of his face had softened, or perhaps relaxed, in the way that faces relaxed when the thing they'd been bracing against had finally arrived and turned out to be survivable.

He'd been testifying. Weeks of depositions, hearings, the grinding procedural machinery of a legal system coming to terms with a phenomenon it didn't have precedent for. He'd been cooperative, articulate, and, Kline reported with grudging respect, genuinely helpful. Because he'd had a change of understanding about who should be making decisions about the Instrument.

Everyone.

He sat in the chair across from her desk, the same chair where Harris Cole had sat months ago, begging her to let him hear the thing that would complete his craving and consume his autonomy. The same chair where Nadia had sat with her box of stolen files. The same chair where a parade of people touched by the sonnet had sat over the course of the investigation, each one carrying a different relationship to a phenomenon that treated every human nervous system as a door and every rhythm as a key.

"You finished the paper," Julian said.

"Published last week. Three journals rejected it. The fourth accepted it with the note that the peer review process had been 'the most contentious in the editor's career.'"

"I imagine it was."

"They don't believe it's possible. Most of them. The neuroscience is solid, they can't argue with the data, but the idea that the human voice, unmediated by technology, can produce the effects I've described..." She shrugged. "It requires a worldview adjustment that most scientists aren't prepared to make."

"Give them time."

"I intend to."

Julian's gaze moved across her desk, across the stacked papers and the laptop and the ceramic cup with its four pens, and came to rest on a single sheet of paper, placed face-up beside her keyboard. He recognized the formatting immediately, the line breaks, the spacing, the visual cadence that distinguished a sonnet from prose.

"May I?" he asked.

Lena nodded.

Julian picked up the page and read it. Silently. His eyes moved across the lines with the practiced speed of a man who had spent his life inside the architecture of this particular verse form, and who could hear the rhythm of the words in his mind the way a conductor could hear a symphony from the score.

He reached the couplet.

Read it.

Read it again.

Then looked up at her with an expression she would remember for the rest of her life, the expression of a man encountering, for the first time, a version of his life's work that he hadn't created, hadn't anticipated, and couldn't have imagined. Not because it was better than his. Because it was *different*. Because it took everything he'd built, every principle, every technique, every century of accumulated refinement, and used it to do something he had never considered possible.

It let go.

"It doesn't end," he said.

"No," Lena replied. "It doesn't."

Julian looked at the page. At the revised couplet. At the two lines that took the sonnet's four-hundred-year trajectory of capture and control and, at the moment of culmination, turned the river.

"This is what you're keeping," he said.

"This is what I'm sharing." She met his eyes. "The original is sealed. Classified. Locked in a facility that I trust more than I trust either of us. The revised version, this one, is the one I'll make available to researchers who want to study the mechanism. If the sonnet is going to exist in the world, and it is, whether we like it or not, then it should exist in a form that teaches the body to let go rather than hold on."

Julian set the page down on the desk with the care he'd once reserved for the most delicate historical fragments in the Order's archive. The care of a man handling something precious.

"You've changed it," he said.

"I've finished it."

He looked at her. For a long time. The kind of long time that only happened between two people who had been through something that no one else would ever fully understand, and who recognized in each other the specific, irreducible mark that the experience had left.

Then he smiled.

It was the smile from the evening in his apartment, the one that had surprised him, the one that belonged to the person underneath the practitioner, underneath the leader, underneath the twenty-three years of precision and control and the desperate, private hope that the thing he built would one day be beautiful enough to reach even him.

"You know," he said, "in four hundred years, no one has ever improved it."

"I didn't improve it," Lena said. "I changed the question."

"From what to what?"

Lena looked at the page. At the revised couplet, with its open ending, its refusal to close, its insistence that the most powerful thing a pattern could do was not capture the listener but set them free.

"The original asks: *What happens when you surrender?*" she said.

She looked at Julian.

"Mine asks: *What happens after?*"

The office held still. The photograph on the wall, Lena laughing, unguarded, human, caught the afternoon light. The city moved outside the window in its unrhythmic, chaotic, beautiful noise.

Julian stood. Reached for his coat. Paused at the door.

"Will I see you again?" he asked.

It was the most uncontrolled thing he'd ever said to her. No cadence. No placement. No architecture. Just a man at a door, asking a woman whether the thing between them had a future tense.

Lena looked at him. At the man who had taught her what her own vulnerability felt like. Who had read her the most dangerous poem in human history because she'd asked him to, and who had wept when she came back from it whole.

"Yes," she said.

Julian nodded. Opened the door. Stepped into the hallway.

Then turned back.

"The couplet," he said. "Will you tell me what it says?"

Lena considered. Then she spoke the last two lines of the revised sonnet, the lines she had written to replace the original's closing trap, the lines that took the oldest known weapon against the human will and turned it into something else.

Something that didn't end.

"So speak me slow, and let the breath move on —

For I am not thy cage... but now thy dawn."

The words settled into the air between them, not with the devastating, capturing, irresistible force of the original couplet, but with something lighter. Something that breathed. Something that opened a door instead of closing one, that pointed toward morning instead of midnight, that left the listener not trapped in a loop of perfect repetition but standing at the beginning of something that hadn't happened yet.

Julian listened.

And for the first time in twenty-three years, for the first time in a life spent perfecting the art of making other people feel things he could never feel himself, Julian Calder felt something.

Not the sonnet's full effect. Not the cascade. Not the warmth and the surrender and the devastating completion that the original's couplet produced in its listeners.

Something smaller.

Something quieter.

Something that lived not in the mechanism of rhythmic entrainment but in the space between two people who had earned each other's trust the hardest possible way.

Hope.

He smiled again, the real one, the unplaced one, the one that belonged to him.

"Dawn," he said.

"Dawn," she confirmed.

He left.

Lena sat in her office, in the quiet, in the afternoon light, and breathed.

Not in iambic pentameter.

Not in deliberate, analytical irregularity.

Just breathing. The way people breathed when they were neither fighting nor surrendering. The way people breathed when they were simply alive, and aware of it, and grateful for the ordinary, extraordinary fact that the next breath was theirs to take however they wanted.

She looked at the revised sonnet on her desk.

Then at the photograph on the wall.

Then at the window, where the world was doing what it always did: moving forward, imperfect and unresolved and full of the specific, beautiful, irreplaceable chaos of things that hadn't been written yet.

She picked up a pen.

And began to write.

• • •

THE END

• • •

About the Author

Heather Hollis writes about influence, and the moments when it stops feeling like influence at all.

At almost thirty and five-nine-and-a-half, broad-shouldered and unhurried, she has the kind of presence that rearranges a room before she opens her mouth. People listen to her. They feel compelled to. It's the eyes, mostly, a calm, direct attention that lands like a hand on the back of your neck, gentle enough to be mistaken for warmth, precise enough to hold you exactly where she wants you. And that smirk. The one that says she already knows what you're going to do, and she's decided to let you think it was your idea.

In her professional life, she works in corporate training, where groups of strangers are expected to learn, adapt, and respond, often in real time. She has developed a reputation for unusual effectiveness. Rooms settle when she speaks. Resistance tends to soften rather than break. People who arrive certain of their positions often find themselves reconsidering, not under pressure, but under something quieter and far more difficult to refuse.

Colleagues have noted, sometimes with visible discomfort, how easily she establishes control without appearing to reach for it. Participants who begin sessions guarded or skeptical often leave having followed her lead further than they intended, with no clear memory of when they stopped resisting. She doesn't negotiate. She doesn't repeat herself. The boundary is set once, and everyone in the room behaves as though they can feel it on their skin.

She is less interested in forcing outcomes than in understanding why people allow themselves to be guided in the first place, why surrender, offered to the right voice in the right moment, can feel less like losing and more like finally being told what you already wanted to hear.

Based near Cleveland and frequently on the road, she studies how context, environment, and the subtlest shift in tone can reshape behavior across settings. Her work, both professional and creative, explores the line between choice and response, and the quiet mechanisms that move that line without anyone noticing it has moved.

She does not raise her voice. She has never needed to.

Sonnet 155: The Velvet Tongue is her debut novel.

www.ingramcontent.com/pod-product-compliance
Lightning Source LLC
LaVergne TN
LVHW020712110826
845149LV00012B/2232

* 9 7 8 1 9 6 6 7 0 3 2 4 2 *